Ruining the Rake

*For June —
Happy reading!*

LEIGH MICHAELS

Leigh Michaels

PBL Limited
Ottumwa, Iowa

Copyright 2014 Leigh Michaels

Cover design copyright 2014 Lynda Gail Alfano
Cover art provided by Fotolia

ISBN 13: 978-1-892689-94-8

All rights reserved. Except for brief passages quoted in any review, the reproduction or utilization of this work in whole or in part, in any form or by any electronic, mechanical, print or other means is forbidden without the written permission of the author.

This is a work of fiction. Characters and events portrayed in this book have no existence outside the imagination of the author. Any resemblance to real persons, living or dead, or real events is purely coincidental.

Ruining the Rake

Acknowledgments

Special thanks to Rachelle Chase, my first reader – whose enthusiasm always makes writing fun. To Lynda Gail Alfano, my cover designer – you are a bright spot in my life. To Elaine Orr, my speedy and careful copy editor -- thank you for all the years of friendship.

And as always, to my readers. You make it all worthwhile.

Chapter 1

The main avenue running through Vauxhall Gardens was lined with lanterns, but only a few steps beyond the path's edge, darkness closed in. Anything – or anyone – might be lurking there, and a shiver ran up Elinor's spine. Despite her best efforts at self-control, impatience colored her voice. "Do come along, Izzy. If we don't hurry to catch up with the group, we'll be left behind."

"And a good thing that would be," Izzy countered, "for then we could actually talk without having to shout over Mary Wishart's bray of a laugh. What she has to giggle about escapes me, anyway."

"I suppose it might be the fact her betrothal is to be announced tomorrow."

Izzy sniffed. "As though being betrothed to a man old enough to be her father is anything to celebrate, even if he is a marquess."

Elinor had to agree with Izzy there. Why, the gulf between Mary and her proposed husband must be every bit as wide as if... as if Elinor herself were expected to wed her elderly guardian's friend, Mr. Dorrance!

"Let's go this way," Izzy went on. "I'm almost certain I remember a little folly just down this way where we can sit for a moment, so you can tell me why you're acting so cabbage-headed tonight."

Cabbage-headed? That's very much a case of the pot insulting the kettle.

Elinor paused to look down the winding path Izzy had indicated. "But it's even darker down there, and it's almost time for the fireworks. I don't wish to miss them."

"Of course it's dark. Shadowy paths are one of the very best things about Vauxhall Gardens. Don't fuss about the fireworks, for you can see them from everywhere inside the walls – and in any case, they're not exactly one of the wonders of the world."

"Perhaps not to you, since you come to Vauxhall so often. But since it might be my only opportunity to see them..."

Izzy started off down the winding path. "Are you coming, or will you leave me completely alone to wander the gardens?"

"If the other girls come back to the pavilion without us, your mother will be extremely unhappy."

"Then come along quickly, so we are not unduly delayed. Or would you rather wait here alone while I go on?"

Elinor muttered under her breath – but though going off into the darkness with Izzy was frightening, the idea of being entirely alone in the unfamiliar maze of paths was even more disturbing. So she caught up her skirt and hurried after her friend. "How far..."

"The folly should be right up ahead. But... oh, bother." Izzy's voice dropped to a whisper. "Someone's already there."

Relief flooded over Elinor; if the folly was already occupied, Izzy would have to give up her plan. "If we turn back now, perhaps we can still catch up with the other girls before they reach the pavilion."

"You just don't want to tell me what's on your mind."

Elinor had to admit Izzy was right. But no matter what Izzy thought, there really was nothing to tell. It was just an odd feeling Elinor had of late – that something important was happening around her, something no one wanted to tell her about. The sensation was enough to make anyone rattlepated, but surely it would turn out to be nothing.

Izzy put a finger across her lips and tiptoed closer to the folly. In the quiet, Elinor could hear voices – the trill of a lady and the deeper, warmer tones of a gentleman.

"You are a shameless flirt," the lady said.

"And you knew that the moment we were introduced, my lady. Yet here you are, alone with me..."

"Don't make me regret it, Lord Rake."

Izzy's eyes widened. "*Lord Rake*? I must get a glimpse."

Before Elinor could even form an objection, Izzy dragged her a few steps closer to the folly, pushing past a bush loaded with white blossoms. Once past the bush, Elinor could see the folly, its roof silvered in the moonlight, as well as the figures of a man and a woman inside, silhouetted against a single lantern illuminating the interior.

"Alas," the lady said, and Elinor not only saw but heard the soft smack of a fan against the gentleman's gloved hand. "Your *tendre* for me is destined to be unsatisfied."

The gentleman seemed not to hear. "Run away with me, Delia."

"Where would you take me, Rake? To Paris?"

"Paris..." Izzy's sigh was little more than a breath.

Intrigued by the conversation, Elinor had almost forgotten her friend. With her manners abruptly recalled, she tugged at Izzy's sleeve and gestured back toward the main avenue and the pavilion.

Izzy shook her head and whispered, "I expect he'll kiss her any minute now, and I want to see what happens."

"Why would you wish to observe such a thing?"

"Have you ever watched?"

"Of course not, but—"

"Annabelle told me that sometimes when a man kisses a woman, he... I'll tell you later. I don't want to miss it." Rapt, Izzy turned her attention back to the folly.

I should leave her right here. But Elinor didn't relish a long walk alone through the confusing pathways.

"Of course we shall go to Paris, my dear," the gentleman called Lord Rake said. "But not for a few months, at least. We'll let the French recover from the havoc Bonaparte caused, before we go. Rather than wait for that day, however, I will take you to Italy first. And then Greece, and Egypt."

The lady sounded doubtful. "I don't care for the idea of Greece and Egypt. And there is the small matter of my husband as well. What if he should discover the plan and challenge you to a duel over my honor?"

"Don't bother your head with him. He'd probably not even chase after us."

"What a sadly unflattering thing to say to a lady, sir – that her husband would not pursue her if she fled with an admirer!"

"I only meant he'd never dare to call me out, for he well knows how the encounter would end."

Elinor wasn't certain how it had happened, for she didn't remember moving – but perhaps Izzy had taken another step forward and Elinor, still clutching her friend's sleeve, had mindlessly shifted along with her.

Suddenly she was close enough that Lord Rake was no longer just a silhouette. The flickering light of the single lantern inside the folly gleamed against his dark hair and made the gem-set buttons on his coat sparkle. To Elinor's dazzled eyes, the glittering buttons looked like diamonds – but what an affectation that would be. To say nothing of how much wealth a man must possess even to dream of such a thing as using jewels for buttons.

The lady shook her head. "They say in the *ton* you

have a silver tongue, my fine Lord Rake, but I think they are sadly mistaken. To insult me in such a way!"

Elinor was close enough to see the slight shake of the gentleman's dark head. "It is certainly unflattering for your husband not to wish to die in defense of your honor. But it's very sensible of him nonetheless, for he is no match for me with pistols or swords, and he knows it well. The truth is, your husband doesn't deserve you."

"He would no doubt agree with you," the lady said thoughtfully, "for he loves me madly and thinks I am far above his touch. How could I possibly turn my back on such devotion as his?"

"What about my devotion to you?"

"You must give it up, Lord Rake, and accept the truth. I shall always belong to another."

"It would serve you right if I took some other lady to Italy and Greece – and Paris – instead of you."

"Oh, just *kiss* her," Izzy implored, under her breath.

The gentleman turned his head and stared directly into Elinor's eyes.

He must have the hearing of a cat.

The light of the single lamp inside the folly caught on the planes of his face, and for an instant, Elinor stood frozen, simply staring at him. Her throat felt tight, and her stomach seemed to simply be gone.

He was not handsome, at least not by this year's standards amongst the *ton*. His hair was nearly black and straight and too long to be stylish, and his eyes were so dark they seemed to have no color at all. Current fashion – as far as Elinor had been able to discern from the few weeks she had spent on the fringes of the *ton* – preferred gentlemen to have blue eyes and light-colored hair arranged in disordered curls.

And yet there was something about this man that kept Elinor standing very still, staring directly at him across the top of a low boxwood hedge. Perhaps it was the passion he so clearly felt for his companion that inspired her, but Elinor almost felt sorry for him. He was clearly a rake, of course, and not only by name. Trying to seduce a married woman into leaving her husband! The idea took her breath away. Still, there was something about him...

She gasped as Izzy almost pulled her off her feet and away from the folly. Elinor realized she had ceased breathing while she stared, and they were almost back to the main path before she fully recovered from the lack of air.

"He saw us," Elinor gasped.

"Not clearly enough to matter. So Lord Rake has fallen in love. Who would have believed it possible? Just wait till I tell Annabelle Knowles."

"Izzy, you cannot mean to brag to *anyone* about how we spied on them!"

"I wouldn't call it spying. I'd call it... oh, reconnoitering, perhaps."

"And why should you intend to tell Annabelle, of all people? I hardly thought you two were bosom-bows."

"Because she's determined to meet him. The silly chit actually believes all she need do is throw herself in Lord Rake's path and he will instantly fall prey to her charms. I was so amused by her pretensions that I wagered my best pearls she could not succeed even in meeting him before the Season ends. Foolish of me, of course."

Elinor's head swam at the notion of Izzy's perfectly-matched double strand of pearls at risk. If she herself possessed anything half so grand, she would never take such a chance. "It certainly *was* foolish!"

Izzy nodded. "She had nothing of nearly as much value to put up, so she staked her mother's Norwich shawl. The trouble is, even though I've won the bet fair and square, it's hardly worth the effort. It's really not a particularly nice shawl, and the color would be all wrong for me."

"It's a relief to know you wouldn't actually collect on such a wager. Think what Annabelle's mother would say, losing her shawl in such a cause."

"Of course I'll collect." Izzy shrugged. "Annabelle shouldn't have staked what she isn't willing to lose. I must say, however, I shall thoroughly enjoy watching her face when I tell her what we discovered tonight. I wonder who the woman was... Bella? Is that what he called her? I don't remember anyone in the *ton* ever mentioning anyone named Bella, but she was clearly a lady."

She was called Delia, Elinor almost said. *Not Bella.* But she caught herself just in time; it was probably better if Izzy didn't have the right name. "Isn't *Bella* what Italian men call any attractive woman? If he's been to Italy before, he might have picked up the habit."

"He was gone all of last Season, so I shouldn't be surprised if he's been to Italy. And she was pretty."

Elinor hadn't noticed. But then Lord Rake had been watching her with a disturbingly direct gaze. Izzy, who hadn't been subjected to his stare, had been free to inspect his companion.

"Well, even without the lady's name," Izzy said, "this is the best piece of tittle-tattle ever."

Elinor couldn't see why. "Who is Lord Rake, anyway, to make him so special?"

"How can you not have heard of him? He must be the most notorious roué in England – even though he seldom goes into polite society."

"Then what a very *apropos* name he has!"

Izzy snorted. "Of course it's not really his name. He's the Earl of Rackham, actually. Don't you know anything?"

Apparently not. Elinor bit her tongue.

"You must at least have heard of Rackham House, on Grosvenor Square... Oh, I do beg your pardon, Elinor. I forgot for an instant this is your first visit to Town, and your family, and your chaperone, are not..." Izzy paused and went on delicately. "Not as well-connected as others are."

Embarrassed color warmed Elinor's face. Though Izzy's words stung, everything she said was indisputably true. Izzy's father was a viscount, her mother the youngest daughter of a very wealthy earl – so Izzy was related to everyone, it seemed.

Elinor's father had been a barely-noticed twig on a baronet's family tree, and her mother's family had been minor gentry. Upon their almost-simultaneous deaths five years ago, they had left Elinor in the custody of a distant relation who was apparently the only family she still had. With no dowry and no expectations, Elinor had anticipated spending her life keeping house for the man she had learned to call Uncle Reginald, who was the squire and justice of the peace in a tiny village in Kent. She had certainly never hoped for a London Season. She had already turned twenty-one and assumed she was too old for the honor.

All of a sudden, however, and only a few weeks ago, Reginald Holcombe had looked up from reading his correspondence at the breakfast table and told her to pack her trunks because they were going to London. Elinor had been too startled, and perhaps too afraid he would change his mind, to ask for explanations.

So here she was – far older than the other girls who were in their first Seasons, and yet far less experienced and knowledgeable than any of them, trying her best to fit in despite her lack of preparation and her very late start.

She didn't even know why Izzy had taken her up. Perhaps their friendship had come about because Elinor wasn't as dewy fresh as the younger maidens were, so Izzy – who was coming to the end of her second Season – looked younger by comparison. Perhaps it was because Elinor's naiveté made her the perfect unwitting partner in Izzy's schemes. Or perhaps it was because other mothers deliberately kept their daughters away from Viscount Arlington's rackety offspring, so Izzy stood as much in need of a friend as Elinor did.

The path they were hurrying along joined in with a wider and even better-lit one, and to Elinor's relief she spotted the pavilion. She wasn't at all looking forward to the scolding they were bound to get, but she was still relieved to be back among the crowds.

She barely listened as Izzy's mother sharpened her tongue regarding her daughter's conduct.

"How can you possibly have become separated from the other young ladies, Isolde?" the viscountess raged. "You gave me such palpitations, I am tempted to send you straight back to the country!"

Elinor's own chaperone – the tall, gaunt, sharp-eyed widow who Elinor's uncle had hired to shepherd her through society's pitfalls – beckoned. Elinor took a deep breath and went to stand beside her chair, her head up and her spine straight. "I have no excuse, Mrs. Whitfield."

The woman gave her a scathing look promising much more to come, but she said, "It's time to go, Elinor."

She wouldn't get to see the fireworks, then. At least not the brilliant, multicolored ones Vauxhall offered. The explosion Elinor suspected she was in for would be of a much different sort.

But as she had learned in the last four weeks, arguing or pleading would only make things worse. "Yes, ma'am," Elinor said. She made her curtsy to Izzy's mother, thanking her for the wonderful and unexpected treat of a trip to Vauxhall, and Viscountess Arlington interrupted her scorching harangue of her daughter just long enough to smile vaguely at Elinor.

As soon as the hired carriage pulled away, Mrs. Whitfield fixed her gaze on her charge. "I am appalled by your behavior, Elinor. When your uncle approached me to ask that I supervise you, he gave me to believe you were a chit who possesses reasonable common sense, but I must say I see no evidence."

Going off by ourselves was Izzy's idea, not mine. But true though the statement was, loyalty to her friend wouldn't allow Elinor to say it. She had chosen to fall in with Izzy's whim; she could have hurried along the prescribed path and caught up with the other girls.

"You will come to regret your lax behavior, Elinor. Miss Arlington can afford to be seen as a hoyden. You cannot."

What Mrs. Whitfield meant, Elinor knew, was that Izzy not only had a well-placed family and a titled father, but a dowry of at least twenty thousand pounds. Therefore, whatever Izzy might do would be greeted with indulgence in the *ton*, while Elinor, who had no such backing or wealth, would be judged much more harshly.

But Elinor's self-control, and her patience with Mrs. Whitfield's never-ending lectures, had worn thin. "As if it matters what I do."

"*What* did you say? Stop nattering, girl, and speak up!"

"I cannot think anyone will take note of my actions," Elinor said quietly. "I am hardly the focus of the *ton*'s attention."

"Spoken like a true greengoose. Of course you're correct. Lady Jersey and Mrs. Drummond-Burrell and their friends will not discuss your antics tonight, for you are beneath their notice. But when the only valuable things you possess are your virtue and your reputation, you cannot risk so much as a breath of scandal. Why, what Mr. Dorrance will think of your behavior tonight, I shudder to contemplate."

"Mr. Dorrance? What, pray tell, does my uncle's good friend have to say in the matter, Mrs. Whitfield?"

For the first time in the four weeks since her uncle had introduced her to Mrs. Whitfield, Elinor saw the woman look uncertain. But by then the carriage was drawing up to the house Uncle Reginald had hired, in a less-than-fashionable neighborhood in Bloomsbury, and Mrs. Whitfield did not answer.

* * *

By morning, Elinor had convinced herself that no matter how annoyed Mrs. Whitfield had been with her after the Vauxhall incident, the woman had simply been issuing mindless threats. A paid chaperone had few options when it came to disciplining her charge; her only real power would be to report Elinor's conduct to her employer.

But by informing Elinor's guardian of his young ward's misbehavior, Mrs. Whitfield would also be confessing that she was unable, in her role as chaperone, to keep her charge in line. Such an admission might lead to the woman's instant dismissal, though Elinor suspected a replacement chaperone would not be easy to find in the last weeks of a London Season. And such an admission wasn't likely to win Mrs. Whitfield a good recommendation or a bonus – either of which must be crucial to a woman in her circumstances.

No, Elinor assured herself. Mrs. Whitfield would keep her own counsel – this time, at least.

But she knew she'd had a lucky escape. It would behoove her to be far more careful in future, particularly when she was in company with Izzy Arlington. She wouldn't actually avoid the young woman, for Elinor's own social standing was hardly secure enough to insult a peer's daughter. But she'd pay a great deal more attention from now on to Mrs. Whitfield's multitude of rules, no matter what Izzy thought of them.

Having resolved to be a model charge for the few weeks remaining of the Season, Elinor went down to breakfast with a relieved mind, a light step, and a smile.

Mrs. Whitfield was seated at the table, a plate of toast and a cup of tea seemingly untouched in front of her.

"Has Uncle Reginald already breakfasted?" Elinor lifted the lid of a chafing dish to see what Cook had sent up this morning. It appeared to be rubbery scrambled eggs again, and she sighed. But then, on the budget her uncle had set for the household, Cook could hardly produce more appetizing fare.

"He has." Mrs. Whitfield's tone was unusually flat.

Elinor turned to look more closely at her. The expression on her chaperone's face puzzled her, for it was a mixture of emotions that seldom coincided. The woman was pale, her jaw set hard as if she'd been on the receiving end of a scold. Yet in her eyes was a glimmer of... could it possibly be satisfaction? Even a dash of glee?

"He wants to speak to you in the library immediately," Mrs. Whitfield went on, and this time there was no doubt about the enjoyment in her tone.

Elinor looked down at the chafing dish of eggs, feeling her stomach turn over. She set her still-empty plate aside, made her curtsy purely from habit, and went downstairs to the tiny room on the ground floor that Uncle Reginald had claimed. Calling it a library was a bit of an embellishment, Elinor thought, since there was just one bookcase and it was scarcely half-full of worn leather-bound volumes of sermons and essays. But since it was his retreat – the spot where he kept up with his correspondence and entertained Mr. Dorrance to the occasional game of chess – she supposed Uncle Reginald was entitled to call the room whatever he liked.

She tapped tentatively, and at Uncle Reginald's gruff summons she went in, closing the door behind her. "You wished to speak with me, Uncle?"

He leaned back in his chair and surveyed her. "I am fond of you, Elinor."

"And I of you," she replied automatically.

"Therefore I had thought to delay this conversation, so you could continue to enjoy yourself for a few last weeks before settling down to marriage."

"Marriage?" Elinor's heart twisted. "I had no notion you intended anything of the sort for me."

"Why did you think we came to London at all, if not to establish you?"

How foolish of her to think the visit had been a mere whim, or a desire to reward her! "This is very sudden."

"Do you think me a fool? Of course it seems sudden to you. It would not be seemly for a young woman to know what arrangements are being considered for her – not until the agreements are worked out and the contracts signed."

So if he was telling her now, did he mean... But surely he couldn't have made such intimate arrangements for her future without even consulting her!

"The formalities were completed last week, but your betrothed was content to allow you a little more time in society."

Since Uncle Reginald seemed to expect some kind of response, Elinor said, "Very considerate of him, I'm sure." Her lips felt stiff.

"His business affairs were pressing at the time, and

there was every reason to allow you to expand your acquaintance in society before the announcement was made. But the latitude you have been granted is at an end, now that the loose behavior you've learned from your acquaintances in the *ton* threatens to ruin your reputation."

Mrs. Whifield told him about last night after all. My instinct was correct; I will never get to see Vauxhall's fireworks.

For an instant, Elinor didn't even realize how foolish it was to regret something as mundane as fireworks when her entire future had been decided without her opinion being solicited. She supposed she had focused on fireworks because the idea of marriage was just too much to take in.

How had Uncle Reginald managed to negotiate a betrothal without her having so much as a hint of his intentions? She'd been in the city only a few weeks, and no man she had met in the *ton* had shown her particular attention or even asked to call on her. Who could this mysterious betrothed be?

"You said – his business affairs?" With an effort, Elinor kept her tone steady. "He is not a gentleman, then?"

Her uncle snorted. "*Gentleman*? I should think not. What an inflated notion of your own worth you must have! The daughter of a penniless vicar can hardly attract the attentions of a gentleman, at least not one who has marriage in mind. I suppose your fairy-tale dream has been to marry some titled twit and become *my lady*?"

Elinor thought for a moment she would faint. "But... you brought me to London. You encouraged me to go into society. You paid for dresses, and for a chaperone, so I could be introduced to the *ton*. Why would you have done all that if you believed it a waste?"

His eyes narrowed. "I need not explain myself to

you, miss – and this hoity-toity attitude of yours is a good part of the reason why you'll be married as soon as the church allows."

That takes three weeks. Sudden relief made her lightheaded. *The banns have to be read out in Sunday services three separate times. Surely I can think of something by then.*

"I comfort myself with the notion that once married, you'll soon learn what's expected of you." Uncle Reginald sounded as if he actually meant to be reassuring. "With a house to run and soon enough a babe or two to nurse, I am persuaded you'll settle down into a model wife."

The house she could handle, of course, because she'd been running her uncle's home for years. But the very idea of a baby... an infant who would be the child of a nameless, formless man... It was a good thing she hadn't eaten breakfast, or her eggs might end up decorating Uncle Reginald's desk.

His gaze sharpened. "Do not think to defy me on this matter, girl."

"Certainly not." *At least not openly, and not now. Not until I've thought up a plan.* Elinor wet her lips. "May I at least be informed, sir, as to who my husband is to be?"

"Didn't I tell you?" Uncle Reginald shuffled papers on his desk. "My good friend, of course – Mr. Dorrance."

* * *

Only Elinor's pride allowed her to stiffly – though mendaciously – thank Uncle Reginald for the care he had taken in arranging her future. She walked out of the library with her head held high and her spine straight.

For just a moment, she had considered flinging herself at his feet and begging. But she knew it would do no good. Reginald Holcombe was of a generation who suspected women possessed no minds at all; he would certainly never consider that Elinor might deserve a say in what happened to her.

She went straight upstairs to the boudoir between her bedroom and the one assigned to Mrs. Whitfield, and stopped on the threshold when she saw her chaperone sitting there already, mending the seam in a glove. But it was too late to back away, so Elinor braced herself for questions.

"I understand felicitations are in order," Mrs. Whitfield said coolly.

"He told you, then?"

"Oh, yes. I have known the plan for some time now. Since the day he hired me, in fact."

"What plan are you referring to, ma'am?"

"Your uncle's plan," Mrs. Whitfield said deliberately, "to bring you to London and dangle you under his friend Mr. Dorrance's nose. Mr. Dorrance never noticed you when he visited Mr. Holcombe in Kent, you know, because there you were only the housekeeper and ward."

"This was his intent all this time?"

Mrs. Whitfield sniffed. "Not such a long time in my estimation. It is my habit to spend an entire Season with a young lady or a family – not to be hired when the spring has already passed and then be let go after only a few weeks."

"You have been let go?" Elinor couldn't say she was sorry, but the move seemed to make no sense.

"As of this morning, yes."

Was it possible the sudden loss of her employment might actually incline Mrs. Whitfield to be a help rather than a hindrance? If only Elinor had some sort of a plan... "He can't have been thinking clearly."

"Mr. Holcombe seemed to know exactly what he was about," Mrs. Whitfield said dryly. "Since you won't be going into society anymore, he says you have no further need of a chaperone."

"But surely he doesn't expect me to stay within the house from now until the..." Elinor couldn't bring herself to utter the word, or to admit there was a wedding hanging over her head. She tried again. "For the next three weeks."

"Three weeks? If he persists in the notion of a special license, your wedding could be as early as tomorrow."

Elinor jerked back as if someone had kicked her in the stomach.

"I did warn you that you would regret your lax behavior," Mrs. Whitfield said. She sounded as if she enjoyed the feel of the words on her tongue. She gathered together the glove and her mending materials and stood up. "I assume the maids will have finished packing my trunk by now, so I must take my leave of you. And Elinor?" Her voice was sickly sweet. "I do so wish you and Mr. Dorrance happy!"

* * *

Spending an evening at Vauxhall was tepid entertainment under the best of circumstances, but Delia had insisted. By the time she'd had enough of the gardens, Augustus Hadley, fourth Earl of Rackham, was too bored and exhausted to move on to other pursuits, so he'd gone home to bed.

The look he had intercepted from his butler when he'd come into the house on Grosvenor Square hours earlier than usual had amused Gus, and then irritated him. Was he really so predictable that any break in his pattern threw his household staff into disarray? Or were his servants so used to him being gone that they were up to no good in his absence?

He made a mental note to check the household

accounts more thoroughly in future, and perhaps to skip an evening at his club now and then just to keep his staff off balance. It was his house, after all, not theirs – every inconvenient niche and awkward corner and drafty corridor and beloved room of it. Perhaps he would even wander all the way downstairs to check out what was going on in the kitchen, and up to the attics to glance into the servants' quarters. He seldom bothered with any area of the house he didn't actually use; that was the sort of thing a wife should keep track of... though he suspected the ladies of the *ton* would rather focus on waltzing at Almack's and paying morning calls.

Yet another item on his list of reasons not to marry.

Early to bed led inevitably to being early to awaken – a good three hours before the time Gus normally roused. He lay still for a while before ringing for his valet, contemplating what he might do with the day that stretched out so unusually long before him. Was Gentleman Jackson in town? An hour spent sparring with the champion might work off his unaccustomed fidgets.

Or he could go look at horses at Tattersall's – though he couldn't fit yet another team of high-steppers into his stables. He had five perfectly-matched sets eating their heads off in the mews behind the Grosvenor Street house already... No, six; he'd forgotten to count the bays. One could, after all, drive only one team at a time, so why buy more of something than one could actually use?

Voicing the sentiment aloud would earn him the reputation of being peculiar. Or perhaps it would be more accurate to say he would be looked on as *even more peculiar*. Who among the gentlemen of the *ton* ever stopped to consider whether he actually needed another team, or another coat, or another carriage, or another house?

"Or even another mistress," Gus said.

His valet looked up from the razors he was laying out on a towel. "My lord?"

"Merely a whimsy, Patchett. Don't mind me."

"I seldom do, my lord."

Gus grinned and set about shaving himself, his hands unusually steady for so early in the day.

As he descended the stairs on his way to breakfast, a commotion at the front door drew his attention. One of the footmen appeared to be attempting to block the entrance as he remonstrated with a caller – certainly an odd circumstance. If it wasn't the master of the house who was the object of the call, the visitor should have used the servants' entrance instead. Gus himself was expecting no visitors, and anyone who had the temerity to call on him at this hour would be such an intimate friend that he would be admitted without question.

The butler hurried toward the door, and Gus's eyebrows rose. He couldn't remember the last time he'd seen old Feather take anything but a slow and deliberate pace. The footman moved aside, deferring to the butler. Beyond him, Gus caught a glimpse of a slight figure draped in an all-concealing dark gray cloak, standing just inside the door.

Gads! Were the determined ladies of the marriage mart pursuing their quarry even into a gentleman's own home these days? Or was this some new sort of wager among the bored young women of the *ton*, to beard Lord Rake in his own den? Last night, there had been those two young ladies prowling around the folly as if they were seeking prey...

"I have come to see Lord Rackham," the visitor said clearly.

Definitely a lady, judging by the accent – though the timbre of her voice was lower and richer than he had expected, not the high-pitched, giggly prattle of the simpering debs whom he avoided at all costs.

Intrigued, he moved closer.

"My business is my own," she said firmly, obviously in answer to a question Gus hadn't heard. "My errand is personal, and I shall speak of it only to his lordship. Please tell *Lord Rake* a lady wishes to see him."

"A lady? Not hardly," the footman breathed with a smirk – until his gaze slid away from the caller and landed on Gus. Instantly, the servant straightened back to attention, displaying the same wooden expression normally found only on a nutcracker.

With the servant reminded of his place, Gus stopped glaring at him and turned his attention back to the gray-clad figure. The cloak enveloped her entire body, and the deep hood was drawn up till it concealed her face. There was nothing he could see about her except her height – or lack of it; he estimated the top of her head would come only to his chin. But her voice...

Gus concluded this was not a woman he'd met before, because he would have remembered her voice. He couldn't possibly have forgotten any woman who could sound so soft, so gentle, and so fiendishly determined – all at the same time.

Regardless of what the footman so obviously thought, Lord Rake had never seduced this female.

Or perhaps it was more accurate to say he hadn't seduced her *yet*. The day was young and he had no other plans, and suddenly Gus felt like whistling.

"Now, Feather," he said gently. "Surely we must not allow a lady to stand on the doorstep where any chance passerby might see." He stepped forward.

The lady turned to face him and curtsied, and for an instant the shapeless, dull-colored cloak parted and Gus was rewarded with a brief glimpse of a pale muslin skirt and a slender ankle.

He swept a magnificent bow. "Do come in, my

dear. I am Rackham – or perhaps I should say, I am Lord Rake. Will you come with me to my library, and tell me what I may do for you?"

He held out a hand, and though she hesitated for an instant, the lady laid her gloved fingers in his and let him lead her across the marble-floored entrance hall. The servants melted away, and as Gus shut the library door, closing them in together, she pushed back the deep hood of the cloak that all this time had shadowed and hidden her face.

He turned to inspect his prize – and sucked in a stunned breath, for this young woman was familiar after all. "You were at Vauxhall last night, at the folly. What the devil are you doing in my house?"

And she said, in her gentle and soft and very determined voice, "I want to run away with you."

Chapter 2

Escaping from her uncle had been no challenge at all. The news of Elinor's situation must have spread through Reginald Holcombe's household as quickly as flames licking at velvet. The servants seemed to share her distaste for Mr. Dorrance, judging by the sympathetic looks and murmurs greeting her in every room.

Furthermore, by a strange coincidence, no one seemed to notice when Elinor, wrapped in her maid's drab gray cloak, slipped through the kitchen and out the back door. Every single servant in the house was occupied elsewhere at that moment — except for Cook, who was absorbed in shaving sugar from the cone and didn't even look up, despite the awkward creak of the door as Elinor opened it.

A hackney providentially pulled up just down the Bloomsbury street from the side entrance where Elinor emerged, and she hung back as the elegant woman inside paid her fare and, after looking around a bit furtively, hurried up to a nearby house. Then Elinor raised a hand to the driver, who walked his horses over to her. "Grosvenor Square, if you please," she said, and managed to climb into the carriage without assistance.

Once she reached the square, the first costermonger she asked was able to point her to Lord Rackham's house. Everything was going so smoothly, in fact, that Elinor had begun to congratulate herself on her plan — until she encountered Lord Rackham's footman and found herself stopped firmly on the doorstep. The manservant might as well have been made of stone for all the sympathy he showed, and Lord Rake's butler was no more understanding. Elinor was starting to panic when the lazy, cultured voice she remembered so well from the folly cut across the butler's questions.

She had thought his voice rich and vibrant on the previous night, as she listened to him flirt with Delia in the folly. But having those low, warm, sultry tones directed toward her was a different thing entirely. She seemed to be melting inside.

Will you come with me to my library?

A lady would not do anything of the sort, of course – she would never go into a private, closed room alone with a gentleman to whom she was not married, or at least betrothed. But then a lady wouldn't have sneaked out of her uncle's house, or taken a hackney carriage without her maid, or knocked on a gentleman's door, or demanded to see him, or called him by his disreputable nickname – so why should she cavil at taking this last step to ruination? It was what she wanted, wasn't it?

Elinor put her hand into Lord Rake's, feeling oddly as though she might need to lean on him to keep her balance. Once they were inside the cool, quiet, dim book-lined room, she pushed back the hood of her cloak.

Perhaps it was the momentary shock in his eyes when he recognized her – quickly concealed, but there nevertheless – that prompted her to be so blunt in stating her intentions. During the night, in the quiet hours when she had found it impossible to sleep, she'd actually planned out their conversation. She would lead up slowly to her request; she would so persuasively explain the bargain she had in mind that he would see all the advantages just as clearly as she did, and he would eagerly agree to her plan.

Instead, the instant he saw and recognized her face, he demanded, "What the devil are you doing here?"

And as though she had no control at all over her tongue, Elinor looked straight into his eyes, just as she had at Vauxhall, and blurted, "I want to run away with you."

For just a moment, he looked as though she had smacked him over the head. So much for her careful plans, her reasoned presentation. She tried to regain her balance. "Last night in the folly the woman you were with refused to go away with you."

"Do you know, I seem to recall that."

She felt as awkward as if her tongue were tied in a knot. "I only meant... I'm trying to lay a foundation here, my lord."

"For what? Am I to conclude you're offering yourself as a substitute?"

The amusement in his voice sent hot color surging over Elinor's face. *Even a rake doesn't find you attractive.* Certainly not when she was compared to a sultry temptress like the one who had been keeping company with him in the folly last night.

Pretty, Izzy had called that woman. But even though Elinor had barely glanced at her – she'd been too caught up in staring at Lord Rake – she had no doubt Izzy had been understating the truth. Delia had been too self-confident to be anything but a beauty.

Besides, a man like Lord Rake would never settle for an ordinary woman – a woman with average brown hair, average brown eyes, average height and figure.

Too late, Elinor caught herself up short. Of course she didn't want him to see her as a possible conquest! Her plan depended on him *not* finding her appealing enough to be intriguing.

She gathered her poise and went on. "You told her it would serve her right if you took some other lady to Italy and Greece – and Paris – instead of escorting her."

"You remember the conversation word for word? Congratulations on your recall. How long had you been eavesdropping, I wonder, to take in all the details?"

Elinor pretended not to hear him. "She did not

appear to take you seriously. I am merely suggesting you make good on what you told her. Where persuasion does not work, a concrete example often does."

"You're suggesting I should carry out my threat? It's quite selfless of you to offer yourself as a sacrificial lamb, by the way." Before Elinor could even bristle, Rackham went to the door and called for the butler.

He's throwing me out – but I won't make it easy for him. He must listen to me... because I don't know what else to do.

She couldn't hear the low-voiced conversation between master and servant, but after a moment Rackham came back to the fire where she had seated herself in a wing chair. Elinor noticed he hadn't quite closed the library door this time. "You needn't be so cautious, my lord. You are in no danger from me."

"It is regrettable I am such a coward, Miss... I don't believe I have been honored with your name."

Elinor hesitated.

"If we are to be traveling companions on the way to... was it Italy that seized your fancy and made you step up with your offer? Or are you, like Delia, holding out for Paris?"

His gently-mocking tone made her skin itch. "Don't be ridiculous. I wasn't suggesting we actually go anywhere." She paused. "I mean, nowhere as far or as complicated as Italy."

"Then I believe I must ask you to explain what it is you *do* mean."

He was actually going to listen? Elinor felt dizzy at the prospect of having every fragment of Lord Rackham's attention focused intently on her. His eyes, she noted, were not black and colorless after all, but a very deep and intense blue – though his hair was every bit as dark and shiny and unruly as it had appeared in the lamplight last night.

"Let's begin with your name," he suggested. "And you will give me the correct one, if you please."

"As though I would lie about my name! I am Miss Elinor Holcombe. My guardian is Reginald Holcombe, a very distant cousin – though since he is quite old, I have always called him uncle. He resides in the village of Camberford, in Kent, where he is squire and justice of the peace."

"Ah. An upstanding citizen, I collect."

"I am quite aware you are laughing at me, my lord. I tell you about my uncle not to be pretentious, for I fully realize his standing does not earn respect in the *ton*, but merely to point out that I am not entirely the foolish upstart you seem to think me."

"You would do a great deal better not to assign ideas to me, Miss Holcombe, for your assumptions may well run astray. Why did you bring up your uncle, if not in a foolish effort to impress me?"

"Because… well, in short, because he has arranged a marriage for me that I do not want and will not consent to."

"Forgive me, Miss Holcombe, but it seems rather a large leap to attempt to run away with a rake simply because you do not wish to marry. Is it the man you object to, or the institution of marriage as a whole?"

"I have never expected to marry. I have no dowry, you see, and no expectations. But now my uncle has chosen a husband for me, a man who wishes to wed me only because of the mistaken belief that having a wife who has some connection with elegant society will increase his business."

Lord Rackham showed faint interest. "What sort of business does this suitor engage in?"

"He is a wine merchant, my lord."

"But he's not successful enough to please you? Or is it because you object to the aroma of trade?"

"His is an honest living, I believe – and no female who is entirely without a portion can consider herself to be above a match with a tradesman. But he is a great deal older than I, and he has said fewer than ten words to me in our entire acquaintance."

He raised an eyebrow. "Perhaps the wine merchant is simply a shy man who does not know how to woo a lady."

"Also," Elinor went on crisply, "he has very little hair, only half his teeth, and a lamentable fondness for eating raw onions. At least, I must assume from the quality of his breath that they are a favorite dish."

"Oh, well. His culinary preferences certainly explain your hesitation to wed him. But why you should wish to drag me into the matter still eludes me."

A tap sounded on the door, and without waiting for permission, the butler marched in with a tray containing a teapot and a single cup and saucer, along with a decanter and two glasses.

"Thank you, Feather," Lord Rackham murmured. "That will be all."

He waited until the butler had gone, leaving the door once more a precise two inches ajar, and then indicated the tray. "Tea? Or will you join me in a glass of burgundy? I wonder if this particular vintage was provided by your betrothed."

"I should think it very unlikely that Mr. Dorrance enjoys your custom, my lord, or the business of any of your friends. If he already had that sort of client, he would not find my position at the very edge of the *ton* to be so attractive."

"How did you meet him?"

"He is a long-time friend of my uncle's who apparently had no thought of marriage at all, until—"

"Until he saw you and was knocked off his feet by your beauty?"

"There is no need to be sarcastic, my lord." Elinor focused her attention on the tray, filling her cup with steaming, fragrant tea to precisely half an inch from the lip. "I was about to say, until he saw me going about in society and listened greedily to my uncle's tales of how much his business could benefit from having a lady to wife. My uncle, it seems, has an unexpected gift for embellishing stories."

"And you know all this because you were eavesdropping on your uncle as well as on me?" He poured wine from the decanter into a glass and took a long swallow.

"Of course not. My chaperone made it a point to tell me the whole as she was taking her leave of the household. She made certain to inform me how my uncle schemed to marry me off as quickly and inexpensively as possible."

He quirked an eyebrow. "By bringing you to London? A Season and all the associated expenses are hardly the miser's way to marry off a ward."

"Uncle Reginald seems to have regarded it in the light of an investment. He had no success with inviting his friend to Kent, you see, for though Mr. Dorrance enjoyed the hospitality of my uncle's house, he showed no interest in me."

"How very insensitive of him. Mr. Dorrance, I mean."

Was that a smile tugging at the corner of his mouth? She could hardly make herself any more ridiculous than she already had, so Elinor plunged on. "My uncle brought me here to throw me once more into his friend's orbit, but this time he also set out to show Mr. Dorrance how my social standing could be worth a great deal to a wine-merchant's business – by dressing me as a lady and sending me into the *ton*."

"If that cloak is an example of your wardrobe," he

said lazily, "I must disagree with Uncle Reginald's ideas of how a lady rigs herself out."

Elinor had forgotten she was still draped in the gray cloak. She untied the strings and laid the wool back over the arms of her chair.

Lord Rackham's gaze slid slowly down over her pale green muslin walking dress.

Elinor felt heat pulse through her, as though the small, neat blaze on the hearth had suddenly flared up and threatened to consume the room.

"That's better," he said. "Not entirely pleasing, I must say, but bearable. Clearly not a big spender when it comes to fripperies, your Uncle Reginald."

"I believe he planned to get double duty from my wardrobe by making it serve as a trousseau as well." Compared to the far larger betrayal, her uncle's petty penny-pinching over her clothing hardly mattered anymore. "Mr. Dorrance took the bait, and Uncle Reginald arranged everything, even the signing of the marriage contracts, before there was any hint to me of his intention."

Lord Rackham refilled his glass and said easily, "I'm horrified, of course, at such behavior." He sounded barely interested. "But if you're expecting me to come to the rescue, I'm not in the habit of doing favors for schoolroom misses."

"I'm not a schoolroom miss, sir. I'm turned twenty-one. And I'm not asking a favor, I'm offering a bargain." Elinor heard the tart note in her voice, and deliberately softened her tone. "So far we've talked mostly about me, but may I remind you there are benefits for you in this plan of mine as well?"

"I am agog to hear what you consider a benefit for me, Miss Holcombe."

At least he was giving her an opening. Elinor wriggled a little in her chair and started from the beginning once more. "Your lady did not seem to take you seriously last night. I am offering to help you win her full attention."

"It doesn't bother you that you'd be assisting in the seduction of a married lady? You seem to have a flexible moral code, Miss Holcombe."

"I would not feel right about suggesting such an action, but since you have both already embarked on that journey, I feel no responsibility for either your downfall or hers."

He shook his head as though puzzled.

"She could have simply refused, you know," Elinor went on reasonably. "Instead, she toyed with you. I am merely suggesting you toy with her in return. If you were actually to carry out your threat..."

"Take another woman to Italy, you mean?"

"*Appear* to take another female with you on your travels."

"You think a bit of tittle-tattle about my plans would change Delia's mind about throwing over her husband and going with me?"

Elinor shrugged. "As matters stand, she believes you enthralled, ready to throw yourself down at her feet no matter how badly she treats you. But if the word were to spread that you have a new *chere amie*, she will regret losing her power over you, and without doubt she will rethink herself. I cannot promise what her ultimate decision will be, of course, but at the very least she will think better of being so flippant in her refusal."

"And I suppose you think it would be a great comfort to me on my travels to know she would remain here in London, wishing she had refused me more politely." He drained his wine glass. "What exactly do you propose, Miss Holcombe?"

Elinor daintily sipped her tea. "I suggest we leave London together, bound – so far as anyone knows – for the coast and then on to foreign parts."

He gave a little snort. "Pursued, no doubt, by your uncle, intent on preserving your honor by forcing a marriage between us. No, that old game won't work on me, miss. I've been playing it far too long to fall victim to a fresh-faced chit."

A fresh-faced chit, am I? She supposed that was better than being the antidote he had seemed to think her. Not that it mattered what he saw in her, of course. "As though I would attempt anything of the sort! If I actually *wanted* to marry, I'd have chosen someone a great deal more..."

"Pliable?" His voice was silky.

Elinor thought it best to change directions. "I believe it unlikely that Uncle Reginald would make even the least effort to follow."

"Are you relying on my reputation with pistols and swords to dissuade him, Miss Holcombe? Don't bother with a denial. You heard everything else I said last night, so you must have heard me boasting of that skill as well."

She shook her head. "I doubt either Uncle Reginald or Mr. Dorrance are aware of your dueling skills, but it doesn't signify in the least. Once a business deal is arranged – and I am certain he regards this as business – Mr. Dorrance is rigid about keeping his word. Unless, of course, it benefits him to break the bargain. That's why I've chosen this particular course of action."

"Because if you exile yourself from society by running away with a rake, you would be worthless to Mr. Dorrance. Therefore he would not hesitate to renege on the marriage contract."

"Exactly."

"But if you've exchanged no more than a dozen words with him, how can you possibly predict what he might do? No, don't tell me – it must be the chaperone again. Where was she when your future was being decided, by the way? Didn't she have anything to say about your uncle's plans?"

Elinor felt strangely reluctant to answer. "Mrs. Whitfield was hired only for the Season." She thought for an instant that Lord Rackham's jaw tightened, and she quickly moved on. "Once it becomes known I have run away with you, Mr. Dorrance will refuse to keep the bargain, my uncle will disown me, and I'll be free."

"Free... but I believe you said, without resources?"

Elinor fidgeted a bit. "Well, I had hoped you'd be grateful enough for my assistance with your little problem that you might..."

"Buy you off? I have never paid for a woman's favors in my life."

She bristled. "I'm not offering my favors!"

"I certainly have no intention of paying you *not* to be my mistress. Come, Miss Holcombe – you must have some actual plan in mind beyond merely escaping a trip to the altar. Surely you didn't devote all this plotting to my situation without giving a thought to your own future."

"Well, it never hurts to ask," she muttered. "In reality, I wish you to take me to Chichester, where my old governess lives now."

"Chichester?" He sounded wary.

"Yes – I believe it's somewhere in Sussex."

"She must not have been a very good governess, if you're uncertain of the location." His voice was dry.

"It's hardly my governess's fault that I never excelled at geography."

"Chichester is very close to Portsmouth, in fact."

"But that's fortunate – because traveling in the direction of the port adds credence to the story that you are taking me to Italy."

"I was thinking it sounded suspiciously

convenient."

"Why? Is Portsmouth where you plan to embark?" Surely he should be pleased – though he didn't sound it.

"'Too convenient by half, in fact."

Elinor bristled. "If you're implying that I chose a destination to match your plans, my lord, let me assure you I am neither knowledgeable nor cunning enough to do so! The fact is my governess is now associated with a school in the city, and I am hopeful..." She steadied her voice. "No, I am certain she can find a place for me, where I can at least earn my keep. Since I have nothing – no inheritance, no dowry, and no particular skills – it seems my best option."

"I wouldn't say you have no skills," he said absently. "As it turns out, you're a formidable negotiator."

For an instant Elinor scarcely dared to believe her ears. "Then – you'll do it?"

"Be warned, Miss Holcombe. If this farradiddle of yours is really a scheme to capture me in parson's mousetrap despite your assurances to the contrary, I assure you I have no intention of ever allowing that to happen."

Elinor was horrified. "I told you it is not! As though I would *want*—" Her voice stuck in her throat, leaving her unable to protest except with a determined shake of her head.

He surveyed her for a long moment and then stood up. "I'll do it. But mind you, only because you're somewhat amusing, and because I find myself at loose ends, with nothing better to do today."

* * *

The way Miss Holcombe's eyes lit up was really quite remarkable, Gus noticed. She was not beautiful –

Delia would put her in the shade without making any effort at all – but when she smiled and those pansy-brown eyes turned momentarily almost to gold, she could be breathtaking.

She was also unusually patient, he noted – sitting quietly with her tea in his library while he set his household at sixes and sevens.

When he went up to his dressing room to change into clothing more suitable for a long trip, his valet ceased folding garments into a pile and stared at his employer for an instant.

"I am merely taking a young lady for a drive, Patchett," Gus said, "so it will do you no good to argue with me."

"I'm sure it never does any good at all, sir," the valet muttered. "But if this is only a drive, why am I packing your small trunk?"

"Oh, I might go on to visit friends for a few days after I drop off the lady. You need not expect me back for a week at least."

Patchett shook his head and muttered, "She can't be up to anything good." But he said it softly enough that Gus could ignore him.

Eventually, Gus was ready, the trunk was packed and carried downstairs, the team of bays was ordered around to the front of the house, and he went back to the library to collect his passenger. He wondered whether Elinor Holcombe was the sort to pace or to fidget. She was probably one or the other, and in either case, he was fairly sure by now she'd be ready to bite his head off. He wondered for a moment if Patchett's instincts were correct. Had Gus's boredom led him into a whim he would soon regret? Spending hours on the road with a termagant for company would hardly be entertaining.

But the young lady had moved into a chair closer to the window, and she was so absorbed in a book that when he cleared his throat to get her attention, she blinked a bit owlishly. "Oh! How foolish of me, sir. I do beg your pardon, but I was enjoying this story so much..." She laid the book aside with obvious regret. "I wish I were able to find out how it ends."

"Bring it along, if you like," Gus said.

She snatched the book up again. "If you really don't mind loaning it to me? I can read as we drive, to make the trip pass more quickly."

She might as well have announced she had no interest in talking to him, which left Gus feeling oddly annoyed for an instant – a sensation that only intensified when he saw the unbelieving stares of two footmen, his valet and the butler as they passed through the entrance hall. Elinor Holcombe walked along with one hand resting lightly on his arm, but she was paying far more attention to the book she was cradling than to the gentleman who escorted her – clearly a fact none of his servants had missed.

Gus drew his driving gloves through his fingers as he watched the footmen carry his trunk out the door. "You have no luggage at all, Miss Holcombe?"

She held up her reticule. "Only this. I could hardly carry a valise."

"I expected your maid would be hovering around somewhere with a hatbox, at least."

"Since I did not want her to bear the brunt of my uncle's disfavor, I left her behind – and I told her, if she is questioned, to say I must have stolen her cloak so I could disguise myself."

Gus eyed the plain gray cloak once more hiding her slender figure. "It is a relief to know that unfortunate garment is not a reflection of your taste."

She tugged impatiently at her hood, and he regretted the impulse to jab at her, when all she'd done was use simple good sense to disguise herself. A maid walking alone on the street was far less likely to be accosted than a young lady who was wandering about with no companion or chaperone.

"I imagine she'll be in disfavor anyway," he pointed out gently. "A maid who doesn't know what her mistress is up to is nearly as culpable as one who's actively involved in the misbehavior."

She sighed. "I expect you're right. But at least Uncle Reginald cannot send her away, for she, along with the rest of the staff, came with the house. And no matter how angry he is, the servants will not have to put up with it for long. With his plans in disarray and Mr. Dorrance no doubt angry with him, my uncle will surely give up the lease and return to Kent as quickly as he can."

Gus led her out the front door and paused on the steps to admire the view. In the street, his new curricle stood gleaming, its black and cream paint catching the sunlight, while the well-rested team of bays stomped impatiently.

Elinor Holcombe stopped dead. "We're going in *that*?"

Gus looked down at her in surprise. She was staring at the curricle as though she'd never seen one before.

Damnation – I should have expected this. He was used to spending hours on the road in an open carriage. He much preferred to be in control of the reins, able to see the road ahead and to breathe freely, rather than riding closed up in the dark and stuffy box that a post-chaise was guaranteed to be. But it would hardly be a wonder if a lady objected to exposing her skin to sun and wind for an entire day.

"We don't have to," Gus said, and could have kicked himself. This was her plot, after all; he was only going along to be amused. If she didn't like his arrangements, she could damned well make her own – and leave him out of it.

She turned to him with luminous eyes. "I've never ridden in a curricle before. I thought I should never have the opportunity. Oh, Lord Rackham, you are the best of... of..."

He waited, intrigued despite himself to hear how she would complete her sentence. *You are the best of... friends?* Surely not. *Pigeons?* That was more like, for he certainly was one, to have allowed himself to be drawn into her scheme. Lovers? No, she'd made perfectly clear that she had not considered such a thing...

And a pity that is, too.

Well, he consoled himself, it would be a long drive to Chichester – and the odds were good that he'd be so eager to reach the end of their adventure that he'd be springing his horses. It was just as well she didn't have designs on him.

Before she got her tongue untangled enough to finish her sentence, Gus's attention had drifted down the square to where a barouche took up a good deal of the street in front of the house next door. A footman stood at attention beside the steps of the carriage.

As Gus debated whether he could safely thread the curricle between the barouche and the hackneys and delivery wagons that always seemed to clog Grosvenor Square, or if he'd have to wait for the barouche to move instead, an old lady dressed in black left the house, leaning on a footman's arm.

Just my luck that the biggest gossip in London lives next door.

But in fact it *was* a piece of luck that his neighbor happened to be departing just then. Since the success of Elinor Holcombe's plan depended on getting the news of their flight spread throughout the *ton* quickly and efficiently, what better way to accomplish the purpose than by letting Lady Stone in on the secret?

He kept his voice low. "If you're not completely convinced about the wisdom of this escapade, Miss Holcombe, now is the moment to say so. It's not too late to back out."

"And miss my opportunity to ride in that gorgeous curricle? I would never... But you're not joking, are you?" She sobered. "The truth is I see no other alternative for me, my lord."

"Very well." With the uncomfortable sensation that he was burning bridges, Gus helped her climb into the curricle and hoisted himself up beside her. Instead of gathering the reins, however, he turned to face her, cupped her chin in his palm, and – as she looked up at him with wide and startled eyes – pressed his lips to hers in a long, warm caress.

"Oh!" she said indistinctly, and though he hadn't intended to do anything of the sort, he couldn't stop himself from deepening the kiss. Her unintentional cooperation allowed his tongue to slip easily into her mouth, tasting and teasing, taking the delightful risk that she might use those sharp-edged white teeth to defend herself... but she didn't. She went lax instead, as though inviting him to do even more.

Gus's head reeled, and for an instant before he regained control and broke off the kiss, he was in danger of falling out of the curricle. Lady Stone, he saw, had bypassed her barouche entirely, left her footman behind, and headed straight toward them. Her ebony walking stick tapped firmly against the pavement, punctuating each step, and her quizzing glass was raised to better focus her beady black gaze on the two of them.

"I wonder," Elinor said faintly, "if that was what Izzy meant."

"Who's Izzy?" Gus hardly heard himself.

Lady Stone stopped beside the curricle and peered

up at them. "Do introduce me, Rake." Her voice was even more raspy than usual.

Gus bowed. "Lady Stone, may I present..." He had to fumble through his memory. Damnation, he couldn't possibly have forgotten the chit's name – could he? "Miss Elinor Holcombe, from Camberford in Kent."

Lady Stone frowned, and Gus could almost see her mental gyrations as she sorted through the roster of English families. The woman seemed to carry a copy of the entire genealogy of England's nobility around in her head – down to the last black sheep, by-blow, and distant cousin.

"Holcombe," Lady Stone said slowly. "From Kent... Then you must be Izzy Arlington's little friend, newly up from the country. Rake, have you gone completely mad?"

Maybe, Gus almost said.

"Where in heaven's name are you off to, anyway? And don't trouble to deny that you're leaving town, because if that's not a trunk I see strapped on the back of your rig, I'm damned."

You probably will be, anyway.

He'd finally accomplished the impossible by startling Lady Stone, only to realize too late that the gleam in her eyes boded nothing good. Surely the old duck wasn't sniffing romance in the air! "Not Gretna, that's for certain," he said hastily.

The old woman chuckled, and for an instant she looked even more than usual like a hawk eying a tasty bit of prey. "Do you think I'm a caper-wit, Rake? If I were to go telling the *ton* you'd eloped to Scotland with a girl who's still wet behind the ears, my nephew would lock me up as demented – and with good reason. So where are you going? You can trust me, you know."

Gus opened his mouth, and Elinor shifted beside him and raised a small hand in protest. He paused, regaining his senses. Had he truly been about to rattle off their destination? What had that kiss done to him, anyway? Nothing of the sort had ever happened to him before.

"I beg your pardon, Lady Stone," he said, "for I know you prefer to possess every detail so no one in the *ton* can put you in the shade. But I assure you, no one knows more than you do about this situation." *Possibly even me.*

Lady Stone's bright black eyes grew even beadier. "Oh, Rake, you foolish boy. It would have been so easy to assure me that you're rushing Miss Holcombe off to visit a sick relative. Not that I would have believed you, of course. But the fact you haven't bothered to tell me an outlandish story leaves me wondering whether you wish me to inform Delia of your mysterious departure. Or perhaps you're making a clumsy attempt to warn me not to tell her anything at all. I don't suppose you plan to clarify your intentions?"

Gus smiled, touched the brim of his hat, gathered up the reins, and called to his groom to let the horses go. The bays surged off down the street as the groom swung himself up lightly onto the back of the curricle, and by mere inches their off wheel missed a wagon loaded with casks of ale.

Elinor clutched at the seat to keep her balance, and Gus expected her to protest mightily at what an inexperienced passenger must have seen as an uncomfortably close call. But she seemed not to notice the exactitude of his driving. Instead she craned her neck to look back at Grosvenor Square. "She's still standing there," she reported. "Watching."

"I would have expected nothing else."

"Who is she?"

"You haven't encountered Lady Stone before? Fortunate girl. She is said to be the best-connected and most unrepentant gossip in London."

"You did that on purpose, didn't you? Do you think she'll really tell Delia that you kissed me in the middle of Grosvenor Square?"

"Possibly even before we have reached Knightsbridge." He feathered his horses around a corner and darted a look at her. "You actually aren't going to ring a peal over me for daring to kiss you?"

"Certainly not. It wasn't as though you meant anything by it."

Gus felt a little deflated. Miss Elinor sounded eerily calm for a young lady who had just received what was certainly her first kiss. But perhaps she had no idea – despite his reputation – that she'd been initiated by a master. "Quite true, but I cannot tell you how relieved I am to know you did not assume more than I intended."

"Yes, yes, you've already made clear your fears that I might have a parson hiding somewhere about my person. Tucked into my reticule, perhaps?" But her voice was calm and her thoughts seemed to have moved on. "You don't think she – Lady Stone, I mean – knows Uncle Reginald, do you?"

"I would be amazed if she doesn't," Gus said wryly.

"Oh. Well, perhaps she won't rush to tell him."

"You said you wanted him to know you had run off with a rake."

"Not until we're safely away."

"You mean you didn't actually leave a letter? You amaze me, Miss Holcombe." The name felt odd on his tongue – the same tongue that just a few minutes ago had been mindlessly tangled with hers. In an effort to distract himself, he shot a glance down at her and realized she'd turned just a bit pink – though not from sun or wind. "You *did*, didn't you?"

"I had to make certain Uncle Reginald knows I'm

ruined, not just hiding myself with a friend." She didn't look at him. "Of course I didn't mention your name."

"Now there's a comfort," Gus said dryly. "Perhaps I should have packed my dueling pistols after all. We'll be stopping in Knightsbridge, by the way."

"Why?" She sounded almost frightened. "You wouldn't..."

"Abandon you there? Tempting as the notion is, you need not fret. I said I would take you to Chichester and take you I shall." He sneaked a look down at her and had to smother a smile at the way she was nibbling at her thumbnail. At least she wasn't holding tight to the seat with both hands anymore.

"But it's a very long drive, isn't it? Hours and hours. We shouldn't delay."

"It's not so long a trip as it would be in a post-chaise. And since your governess is not anticipating your arrival at all, she cannot possibly be worried if you are late."

Or if you don't arrive at all. Perhaps I'll just keep you.

Now where had that notion come from? Only an odd whim, he assured himself. No doubt by the time they were within reach of Chichester sometime late in the afternoon, he'd be eager to drop her off at her governess's school and drive away, free once more.

"What's in Knightsbridge, anyway?" she asked.

"Possibly the best mantua-maker in London. You can hardly go to your governess begging for assistance and possessing only the shift you stand in."

"My lord!" Her tone was frosty.

He almost laughed at her – at the absurdity that she hadn't turned a hair at being kissed, but she was irate at the mere mention of underclothing. "If you're objecting to the fact that I know what a lady wears under her gown, then you chose the wrong man to run away with."

She was silent, and he sneaked a look away from

the road. She'd stopped biting her nails, but her small white teeth had closed over her bottom lip, and Gus wanted very much to smooth away the marks she was likely to leave on her flawlessly-plump, perfectly-shaped, tasty, tempting little...

A shout snapped his attention back to his driving just in time as the bays shied away from a lumber wagon.

"I have only a few shillings," she admitted. "I cannot afford clothing until I have a position and a few coins to call my own, so this dress will have to do."

"I assumed your uncle is not the sort to be generous with pin money. Fortunately, I drew out a sum from my bank only yesterday."

"I cannot allow you to purchase personal things for me."

"Then keep in mind that I am only pleasing myself. If I have to ride all the way to Chichester next to that abominable cloak, I shall not be responsible for anything I say."

"Since you already seem to have difficulty keeping yourself from saying inappropriate things..."

And doing them, too. Long minutes after their brief kiss, he could still taste her, as though her essence lingered on his lips. "It's the cloak's fault," he murmured. "I'm hardly responsible for anything I say."

At least she stopped arguing, which was a point in her favor. A female who knew when to concede the discussion was rare, in Gus's experience.

A few minutes later he drew up the curricle on a narrow street fronted with shop windows. The groom leaped from his perch at the back and ran around to take the horses' heads. Gus climbed down and turned to help Elinor. But she sat still, and her eyes were troubled.

I've never before known a woman who wasn't eager to spend money – no matter who it belonged to – on clothes.

He considered tactics. Pleading wasn't his style, and it would be a bad precedent. Besides, begging seemed unlikely to be effective where Elinor Holcombe was concerned. "We'll send the bill to your uncle, brat."

She gave a little spurt of laughter that made her eyes glint almost gold in the sunlight. Before she could argue, Gus swept her out of the curricle and into the shop, where the assistant took one look at the stylish cut of his driving coat and ran to get her employer.

The dressmaker came in a few moments later, her step unhurried. "Good day, Rake. What brings you out at this hour of the morning?"

"Hello, Maria." Gus stepped aside.

Maria's gaze fell on the young woman standing behind him, and her eyes narrowed. "Not your usual style, is she?"

"The young lady requires a minimal wardrobe. Whatever you can put together in an hour." Gus pulled out a handful of coins and stood carelessly jingling them. "I shall make it worth your while. Unless you would rather I take my business elsewhere?"

* * *

Elinor couldn't make up her mind what part of this she hated worst. Having to accept Lord Rackham's charity, which her pride refused to find palatable. Allowing a gentleman to purchase clothing for her, which any lady of quality would find a horrifying prospect. Or standing in Maria's dressing room in her shift while the dressmaker poked and pulled and, it seemed, deliberately stuck her with pins.

Why had she not managed to bring at least a few of her own clothes with her? They could be well on the way to Chichester by now, instead of wasting time in this useless pursuit – for it seemed to Elinor that if Maria managed to produce any garments at all, she would make certain they were ill-fitting and in the least-flattering colors.

But she must have underestimated the amount of silver clinking in Lord Rackham's palm, because as soon as the measuring was completed, Maria issued a few clipped orders to her assistant and within minutes gowns and chemises began appearing. When a second assistant came in with stockings and gloves, Elinor was startled by the variety.

The dressmaker said spitefully, "Are you surprised to find you're not the first woman he's brought to me to outfit? And he prefers not to waste time with multiple shops in order to get everything his *inamorata* needs."

Since Elinor didn't think the woman would believe her, she didn't bother denying the charge that she was another of Lord Rackham's mistresses. "It's very thoughtful of you to provide everything," she said. *To say nothing of profitable.* She surveyed a bright pink gown with a skirt composed entirely of flounces. "But I'd look like a pudding in that. I don't suppose you have anything plainer?"

"Rake doesn't like plain things."

Elinor fixed the woman with a long look. "I do not dress to please Lord Rackham."

Maria's eyebrows went up, but she snapped her fingers at the assistant, and when the young woman came back, she carried a deep blue walking dress, severely tailored and almost plain. "This is much more the thing," Elinor said, and when the dress actually fit, she felt vindicated.

They managed to crush everything into a single bandbox, and Elinor carried it out of the fitting room to where Lord Rackham was lounging in a low chair, a wine glass dangling negligently between his fingers. He checked his pocket watch and stood up. "Finished already? You amaze me, my dear."

"Maria was quite helpful in satisfying my needs." *Thereby doubling the size of my wardrobe. Of course, that's not saying much.* But Elinor wasn't about to be drawn into a discussion in front of the dressmaker about where she was going or what sort of clothing she would actually need. "Oh – I forgot about a cloak."

"Already taken care of." He picked up a pile of fabric in the chair next to him, and the cloak's hem cascaded to the floor in a sweep of golden brown wool. The deep hood and detailed stitching was in the latest mode, and the fasteners at the throat were made of gold.

"It's far too grand and fancy," Elinor protested.

Rackham shrugged. "It's the only one she has. To be fair, this part of your wardrobe should be my choice, since I'm the one who will have to look at it all day. Where is your uncle's house located, by the way?"

"Why do you wish to know?"

"So I can send your maid's cloak back to her." He tipped his head toward an assistant, who was holding a bundle wrapped in brown paper.

"It's on Bedford Place, just off Russell Square," Elinor said. "Mr. Holcombe's house. Her name is Sarah."

Rackham dropped a coin in the girl's hand. "See she gets it today, mind."

"It's very kind of you," Elinor murmured as they returned to the street. "Making certain that Sarah is not deprived of her only wrap. I did give her mine in exchange, but..."

"But you're afraid Uncle Reginald can't be relied on not to seize it from her, since he's the one who paid for it."

"Yes, exactly."

"Then it is just as well that I found it unbearable to look at Sarah's garment."

His tone was light, as though he had done nothing

at all.

"I do thank you, sir," she said as the curricle rolled up in front of the shop. "And when I am able to repay you..." She expected he might argue, or point out the reality that it would be a very long time, considering the situation she was going into, before she possessed sufficient extra coins to reimburse all he had spent. But he only nodded gravely, obviously aware of how much her pride stung at the moment and what a blow she had taken to her dignity, and handed her up into the curricle.

No wonder he's such a success with the ladies. He's very kind... and I imagine they like it when he kisses them, too.

Elinor had done her best for an entire hour not to think about the kiss. It had meant nothing; it had been only a way to start the gossip churning faster.

But now that she wasn't being constantly poked by pins or by Maria's sharp, jealous-sounding tone, she could think of almost nothing else. Her lips still seemed to burn from the heat of his mouth. The taste of him – with a hint of the wine he had drunk in his library as she argued in favor of her plan – still tingled against her tongue.

I will not think about kissing him.

She tried to turn her thoughts elsewhere, recalling the rapt look on Lady Stone's face as she found herself in the midst of a neighborhood scandal, and the stunned expression on the face of Lord Rackham's footman as he stared at them from the half-open front door.

But thinking about the reactions of others was nearly as bad as thinking about the kiss.

Half a minute, perhaps – the kiss had certainly lasted no longer. But it had been a half-minute that would burn in Elinor's memory forever, a half-minute when she had felt treasured and special and beautiful...

I will not think about kissing him!

Perhaps she could distract herself by remembering

the friends she was leaving behind. Not that there were many; only Izzy would miss her.

Izzy – who would be so envious she wouldn't be able to speak when she found out Elinor had not only met Lord Rake but actually been kissed by him... and in public, no less.

Elinor lost herself for a moment in daydreams of how much fun it would be to tell Izzy all the details. How he had looked at her, his deep blue eyes so intense, right before he had turned her face up to his. How his hand had cupped her cheek as gently as if he cradled a flower. How his mouth had brushed against hers lightly at first, before growing firmer and more demanding. How his tongue had teased against her lips, and how very good he had tasted...

Izzy had heard vague stories about kisses, but Elinor could speak from experience – if she chose. But of course she would never tell Izzy. This was private – something she would hug to herself.

In any case, there would be no opportunity. Leaving London in this way meant she would never again be allowed to have contact with a viscount's daughter. Elinor's actions this morning – even without the kiss – had put her truly beyond the pale. She was no longer fit to associate with a young lady of quality, even a rackety one like Izzy Arlington.

But at least I know what it's like to be kissed.

She settled back in her seat with a little sigh of satisfaction.

"Bored already?" Lord Rackham asked. He flicked his whip above the horses' backs as Knightsbridge fell behind them, and the bays lengthened their stride.

Elinor laughed. "Hardly. It feels as if we're flying!"

"Wait till we're truly out in the countryside, and I'll show you what my team can do. These boys have been eating their heads off in the stable, and they need a good run."

"I do thank you for this adventure, my lord. Uncle Reginald thinks curricles are unsafe. They are too easily overturned, he says."

"Only if the driver doesn't know what he's doing."

"And I am quite certain Mr. Dorrance would consider such a purchase to be wasteful in the extreme."

"I hope never to meet Mr. Dorrance. I fear we should not suit."

The very notion of the two of them sitting down to chat was ridiculous in the extreme. "I am truly grateful, my lord. If it were not for you, I should never have experienced this treat."

"I am honored indeed by your company," he said dryly, but she could hear a smile in his voice. "It might be as well, you know, if you would stop calling me *my lord*. Surely if we were in fact running away together, we would be on more intimate terms."

"Are you suggesting I call you *Rake*?"

"Most of my acquaintances do."

Delia had done so, in the folly last night. And Lady Stone, and even the mantua-maker. But it didn't feel right somehow for Elinor to refer to him by the nickname. Though perhaps that was why he was suggesting it? To make certain she didn't forget that even though he had behaved like a perfect gentleman to her – well, other than that kiss, and he'd had his reasons – he could be anything but a gentleman under different circumstances.

Not that she needed to fear such conduct from him, for it was perfectly clear to Elinor that Lord Rackham had a discriminating eye when it came to women. He would have no need to settle for just any female who crossed his path, simply because the one he most wanted was not available.

There was something in her line of reasoning that

she needed to think through in more depth, Elinor realized – just as the first cold drop of rain hit the tip of her nose. She squeaked at the impact and looked up at the sky.

The new wool cloak had kept her warm from neck to toes, and she'd been absorbed in watching the horses and enjoying the passing scenery. She hadn't noticed the sky clouding over and the breeze growing sharper against her face.

"If we're fortunate, we should just skirt the edge of the rain," Lord Rackham said. But Elinor noted a tiny line between his brows.

"I won't melt in a little shower. It was only the suddenness of the first drop that startled me." She eyed the clouds and prudently tucked the book she had borrowed from his library inside the bandbox at her feet.

"You're not going to read after all?"

"You know perfectly well I expected to be cooped up in a closed carriage. Why you even let me bring the book—"

"Keep it if you like. A remembrance of the trip."

As though she would need a reminder of this adventure – not only of escaping London and Mr. Dorrance, but of Rackham himself. But Elinor was quite certain his sense of consequence needed no encouragement, so she pressed her lips together to keep silent – and tasted him once more.

The sky grew darker, and more drops fell. From his perch on the back of the curricle, the groom began to mutter. Elinor pulled her hood more closely around her face and watched water bead on the fine wool of her cloak. A few drops ran along the brim of Lord Rackham's hat and dripped on the layers of capes draping his driving coat, but he seemed not to notice. All his attention was on the road.

The clouds roiled above them and the rain grew

heavier. When lightning speared through the sky, barely missing a church tower in a village just a half-mile ahead of them, the groom swore and darted a look at Elinor. "Beg pardon, miss."

"You make your point as eloquently as ever, Jenkins," Lord Rackham said without taking his gaze off the road. "We'll pull in at the Blue Bull and wait for the rain to let up."

Elinor was relieved, because the last bolt of lightning had been awfully close and surely the high carriage made them something of a target. But she also found herself wishing they didn't have to stop. She didn't quite know why, but a little niggle deep inside her warned that drawing out this trip would be a uniquely bad idea.

She wasn't afraid of Rackham, who had been nothing but kind and generous and gentlemanly. And she'd never been afraid of what Uncle Reginald might do; by now he had probably finished cursing and moved on to washing his hands of her.

She wasn't even certain what she was feeling was actually fear at all. Perhaps it was more a bone-deep certainty that the sooner she reached Chichester and the safety of Miss Bradshaw's company, the better off she would be.

"You needn't stop on my account." But the moment Elinor opened her mouth, the wind whipped a cold splash of rain across her face. The drops felt icy against her tongue. The road gleamed; the surface was no longer simply spattered with rain but entirely wet. The high wheels of the curricle began to gather mud, and when a glob broke free and splattered the shoulder of her new cloak, she couldn't keep herself from exclaiming in annoyance.

Lord Rackham drew the horses back to a walk. "Anyway, I've been thinking fondly of food for a half-hour now."

They were near enough to the village that within minutes the curricle rolled through the gates into the inn's yard. Ostlers came running as he turned the team over to the groom. "See the bays are taken care of, Jenkins, and then get yourself some breakfast."

The groom muttered, "Some of us had our morning meal hours ago."

Lord Rackham grinned. "Then you may consider it in the nature of a bonus."

Once back on the ground, Elinor felt herself still swaying as though compensating for the motion of the carriage. Her cloak, which had seemed so light that the wool drifted around her, weighed her down now that the fabric was wet, and she had to admit the warm, dry, and well-lighted inn was welcome indeed. She didn't realize how chilled she was until she stood by the fire in the private parlor Lord Rackham had commandeered and he gently removed her cloak and sent it off with a housemaid to be cleaned and dried.

Elinor shivered a little under his touch and held out her hands to the fire. He still stood behind her, close enough that if she were to turn around, she would be almost pressed against him. The sheer size of him – tall and broad-shouldered as he was – made her feel tiny and fragile.

She had been alone with him in his library this morning and felt no more than a tingle of excitement because such privacy was forbidden. But being closed into the little parlor in his company was different. Perhaps it was because the inn was more anonymous; though the innkeeper clearly recognized Rackham, he'd acknowledged Elinor only with a polite nod.

Or perhaps the ripple of agitation she was feeling now – the sense that her insides had fermented – was because when they'd been alone and private together in his house, he hadn't yet kissed her...

Oh, do stop thinking about that kiss!

She wondered what Izzy would have thought, had she – rather than Lady Stone – been in Grosvenor Square to observe. Would Izzy have noticed the way his mouth had moved against Elinor's, and how his tongue had slipped so naturally between her lips?

Elinor had not anticipated anything of the sort. The only kisses she remembered receiving were the rare ones her parents had bestowed – her father's lips dry and firm against her forehead, her mother's warm on her cheek. Had she ever given it a moment's consideration, she would have expected a kiss from a man to be much the same.

But then Lord Rackham – *Lord Rake* – was not just any man.

She wondered if it was the business about the tongues that Izzy had heard, or if there was still more about kissing that she didn't know. Of course, she wouldn't be finding out.

And it was utterly foolish – as well as simply wrong – to feel a quiver of disappointment about *that*.

She realized that he'd said something about breakfast, and she turned her head to look at him. From this angle, his lips seemed just right for his chiseled face – a fitting match for the firm jaw, brilliant eyes, and notable nose.

Who would think, in looking at him, that his mouth could be so unexpectedly soft? It could caress like the brush of the softest silk. Elinor felt herself swaying again, leaning toward him.

"Come and sit down," he said. "A cup of tea will fix you up, and you'll get your land legs back quickly."

Elinor thought it unlikely that her unsteadiness stemmed from the motion of the carriage, but she wasn't about to admit how much he had unsettled her. She took a seat at the small table. She'd been too absorbed to notice when the maid had brought in the tray, but the scent of the steaming tea tugged at her senses as she poured.

Rackham shook his head when she offered him a cup. "The innkeeper is bringing me a tankard of ale. I hope it doesn't take long for breakfast to arrive, for fresh air always makes me ravenous."

And that was the sum total of his concerns at the moment, Elinor reminded, and had to laugh at her own foolishness for expecting that inconvenient thoughts about kissing might cloud the experienced Lord Rackham's brain!

* * *

Her laugh startled Gus. The sound was nothing like the affected giggles of the debutantes who had tried to impress him, on the rare occasions when he couldn't avoid them altogether. Elinor's laugh was actually a throaty chuckle, a sort of gurgle requiring the listener to laugh along with her even if he didn't understand the joke. "Are you amused by my plight?" he teased. "How very callous of you to laugh at a starving man."

"A man of such substance as you will hardly succumb in the next few minutes, my lord. But if you should do so, may I have your permission to take your curricle on to Chichester? Your groom can drive it for me."

He stared at her for a moment and then grinned. "You're a right 'un, you know. A good sport. Many a lady would have begun complaining long before the rain started."

"What point would there be in making a fuss? You're not responsible for the storm – and you did give me the choice, back in Grosvenor Square, of calling for a post-chaise instead, so it would be hardly fair of me to carry on about it now."

"That usually doesn't stop the ladies from raising a ruckus."

"You force me to admit, sir, that certain influential personages do not consider me to be a lady. Perhaps they are right. If it is a choice between being here in this comfortable inn with you or being in London with Mr. Dorrance about to call..."

He bowed deeply. "I am humbled by the extent of your regard for me."

She pursed her lips for a moment, and Gus wondered if she had any idea how very kissable she looked. "Oh. It wasn't very flattering of me to compare you with him, was it?"

"It was not."

He was beginning to recognize the way her eyes twinkled in the instant before she made some particularly outrageous statement. "I was merely trying to put you at ease. You would not have liked it if I had made over you, relishing my good fortune in being here entirely alone with you – where I might work my wiles to compromise you and end up as Lady Rackham!"

"You wouldn't know a wile if it bit you, Elinor," he said dryly, "much less know how to work them."

"I see you are taking your own advice about pretending to be on intimate terms – Rake." She gave the name a sort of ironic twist and shook her head. "No, my lord – calling you *Rake* is not comfortable. Besides, if you can use my given name, why should I not use yours? What is it, pray tell?"

"Augustus, if you must know."

To Gus's relief, the innkeeper brought in the ale, and the maid returned with a tray of fresh bread and sliced meats and a single boiled egg standing on end in a china cup.

Gus detected a tiny, almost ladylike growl of the stomach from his companion.

She colored a little and said hastily, "I was too anxious to be hungry this morning."

"But you still laughed at me for wanting my breakfast."

"That wasn't what amused me." But she didn't explain. Instead she concentrated on her egg, tapping her knife around the shell, removing the top, and daintily spooning up the contents. As Gus was demolishing his third slice of beef, she sat back in her chair. "Augustus? It seems no better a fit for you than Rake is."

Gus wondered if he might provoke her into another laugh. "I believe I am offended that you don't find me the autocratic, imperial sort suited to ruling Rome."

"You're autocratic, certainly. But I was thinking more of the Duke of Sussex."

"Prince Augustus the libertine? I must feel flattered, I suppose, that you see no similarity between us."

"Oh, I wouldn't go so far," she murmured. "There seems to be such a fine line between a libertine and a mere rake... Has the storm eased, or am I simply growing accustomed to the sound of rain?"

"It's not slapping against the windows anymore. Once the sun comes out, the surface should dry quickly and we can be on our way."

"I wish I had brought my book in to help pass the time," she mused.

How Lady Stone would laugh at the picture of a female who would rather read than spend the afternoon flirting with Lord Rake.

If you need a way to pass the time, I have a few suggestions... and books are not among them.

He was tempted to invite Elinor over to the settee

for another lesson in kissing – or perhaps an entire afternoon of much more advanced instruction. The rain and the roads be damned!

He sternly repressed the urge. A more experienced woman would expect no more than a few hours' entertainment. But dallying with virgins never ended well, and the last thing Gus needed was an innocent who thought an afternoon's lovemaking should lead to more, and becoming a pest.

But that was hardly likely to be the case with Elinor. Once he'd delivered her into the hands of her governess, he would never hear from her again. Stuck in the wilds of Sussex, confined to the grounds of a girls' school and always under the watchful eyes of the instructors, she'd be in no position to pursue him. And she wouldn't risk her hard-earned place by uttering a word, either – for to accuse him would just as surely ruin her.

Perhaps he *should* instruct her in the finer points of making love. She was going off to a very dull existence; perhaps she'd like to have an afternoon she would never forget...

He cast a glance at the hard, upright settee and thought better of the notion.

"It will be all right, in the curricle, won't it?"

He had to think for a moment about what she meant. *What will be all right? Kissing? Oh. She's talking about the damned book again.* "Of all the things in your bandbox, I should think that would be the one you'd least concern yourself over."

"It's because the book belongs to you," she said readily. "Though I suppose, since you're the one who paid Maria, all of the things she supplied are technically yours as well. Or do you mean that I need not worry, since a thief would prefer to take something easier to sell than a book?"

Gus, caught up in the image of himself as the owner of nearly every stitch of clothing she possessed, was barely listening. If he didn't move quickly, he was apt to sweep her off to the settee, no matter how difficult it would be to find a comfortable position there. He needed to get away. Yes, that was the ticket.

"Something like that," he muttered, and pushed his chair back. "I'm going out to check the road. There's no need for you to hurry. Enjoy the rest of your tea."

And if the road is too muddy to leave here, I'll be in the taproom with my ale. Probably a lot of ale.

Though the rain had come down hard, it hadn't lasted long, and only the top inch of soil was wet through. The road was full of furrows and channels where the last few carriages to pass had churned the mud, but if they took it slowly, they might have easier travel now than would be the case after the sun came out and hardened the ruts.

Eying the sky, as blue and clear to the west as though there had never been a storm, he turned back toward the inn.

He paused with his hand on the door latch as the sodden slap of hooves hitting wet soil drew his attention back to the road. A panting, mud-smeared mare pulled up in front of the inn and stood with her head down, blowing hard. The rider, a bulky man much shorter than Gus, swung down stiffly and dropped the reins in the mud, apparently in too big a hurry even to wait for an ostler to take charge.

Not that the horse was likely to wander off, in her condition.

"Going in?" the rider asked harshly. "Or are you planning to stand on the doorstep for a while longer?"

Gus stepped back and flourished an ironic half-bow. "Go ahead, sir. You're obviously in more of a rush than I am."

The rider nodded civilly enough, as though getting his own way had made him feel gracious for a change. But before he had passed entirely through the door he began shouting for the innkeeper. Gus waited till an ostler had led the mare safely away before he followed. If he had any good fortune at all, the obnoxious guest would have already have found his way to whatever it was he'd been seeking, and Gus wouldn't have to encounter him again.

But his luck had failed. The rider had stopped just inside the door to face the innkeeper, who was fresh from the taproom and still wiping his hands on his apron.

"I'm searching for my young ward," the rider said. "She went missing this morning in London."

Gus's head snapped up before he could stop himself, and the innkeeper darted a look at him.

"I have reason to believe she's traveling in this direction," the rider went on. "Have you seen a young female? About twenty years old, and about this tall." He held a hand at the level of his own nose. "She has brown hair and brown eyes, and she's wearing a gray cloak."

Uncle Reginald in the flesh – and in hot pursuit. So Elinor had been wrong about how he would react to her disappearance.

Or had Gus's initial instincts been correct, and this had been her plan all along? – to get herself compromised, rescued by her guardian, and married off before the poor bamboozled rake knew what kind of trap he had stepped into?

But she couldn't possibly have planned that they would break their journey here, at this unlikely little inn. This wasn't even the town where post-chaises usually stopped to change horses. If not for the rain, Gus wouldn't even have slowed his team to sweep through this village.

And she suggested we go on, didn't she? I wonder if she had a destination in mind where Uncle Reginald was to stumble across us...But then why is he here?

It wouldn't have done her any good to have planned such a meeting. Even if they hadn't stopped in this obscure village, her scheme would have gone awry. She couldn't possibly know that on any journey Gus normally passed straight through the first posting stop. He didn't add horses to his stables unless they were good for at least two stages in the hands of a skilled driver.

But right now it didn't matter whether Elinor was telling the truth or if her entire story had been a ruse. Whether Uncle Reginald really was the outraged guardian or he was only playing the role, the outcome would be the same if he were to find Elinor snuggled in the Earl of Rackham's private parlor.

"She'll be traveling alone," Uncle Reginald went on impatiently. "She has some kind of prank in mind, but the foolish chit will ruin herself if I don't catch up with her."

An onlooker in the taproom door gasped and shook his head. "What young people do these days is sinful."

"Let me think..." The innkeeper's gaze slid slowly back to Gus, who gave the tiniest side-to-side jerk of his head.

Better to be shaken down by a tradesman than end up leg-shackled because of a hot-headed guardian. Or a cold-blooded one, for that matter.

"A young lady," the innkeeper said, and Gus held his breath. "Traveling alone... No, I haven't seen anything of the sort."

Gus intervened before any of the inn's other guests could speak up. "May I ask, sir – if your ward went missing in London, what makes you think she is on this particular road?"

Uncle Reginald glared. "I am acting on information received – though it's none of your business. I'm checking every inn that lies along this route." He shook his finger at the innkeeper. "I'll have you know I'm a justice of the peace, so if you've lied to me—"

The innkeeper held up a hand. "I swear on my mother's grave, I spoke only the truth."

And he had – since Elinor wasn't traveling alone. Gus had to admire the man's smooth delivery.

Uncle Reginald went out, calling loudly for another horse. Only when the sound of rapid hoofbeats died away in the distance did Gus turn to the innkeeper. "I think this will cover my account," he said lightly, dropping a handful of gold into the man's palm.

"Indeed, sir. Happy to be of service." The coins vanished under the dingy apron with the speed of a conjurer's trick. "You and your ... companion . . . will be on your way, I imagine, now the rain has stopped?"

"And before our obnoxious friend thinks better of your elusive answer and comes back to quiz you further," Gus agreed. He took a deep breath and returned to the parlor to find Elinor curled on the settee, apparently asleep.

The gentle curve of her body and the soft rise and fall of her breast made the rigid piece of furniture look inviting. No – the girl herself was inviting; the furniture remained more of a challenge than Gus wanted to deal with. If only it had been a soft chaise instead...

But what was he thinking? With the scent of Reginald Holcombe's cologne – mixed with his angry sweat – still hanging by the inn's front door, how could Gus be contemplating debauching the man's young ward?

Because she looks so very appealing, that's why.

Was it possible her vulnerable pose was by design?

Was Elinor some sort of temptress after all, and not the innocent she appeared?

No, for she would have given herself away when he kissed her. No experienced woman could have held out against the way he had caressed her, but Elinor's response had been unstudied, inexpert – and too willing for his peace of mind. Another few seconds and she would have melted into him.

He leaned over her, studying the curving sweep of her dark eyelashes and the shadows the firelight threw across her fresh, dewy skin.

He caught himself just as he reached out to caress her cheek, and instead he tugged at a curl, harder than he'd intended. "Time to go. By the way, I seem to remember you said Uncle Reginald was elderly."

Elinor's eyelids fluttered, and Gus found himself looking down into great pools of brown – with no gold flashes at all just now.

She sat up slowly. "Did I fall asleep? Uncle Reginald has always seemed and acted elderly, but I suppose he's actually about sixty. Why do you ask?"

"Because he just rode in on a nice mare – at least, she was probably a perfectly good mount before he got hold of her – and he seemed anything but doddering and tottery."

She licked her lips as if they'd suddenly gone dry. "He's *here*?"

"Not any longer. The innkeeper sent him on his way." He kept a close eye on her, watching her reaction. If she showed the least inclination to be upset that her guardian hadn't burst in to save her...

Her eyes narrowed. "But how could he have found us?"

"What did you say in your letter, pray tell?"

"Only that I was going far away with a gentleman who would look after me, and he need not concern himself further because I preferred complete ruin to his idea of a good marriage."

"He doesn't seem to have been convinced, for he told the innkeeper you were likely traveling alone. I suppose you confided your plans to your maid."

"Of course not. I am far from addlepated." She gave a little sniff. "Do you know, it's not very flattering of Uncle Reginald to think no man would offer me *carte blanche*."

"He must believe you were only trying to throw him off the scent by claiming a lover. I assume he knows you had a governess once?"

Elinor nodded. "She was the one who brought me to Kent after my parents died. She only stayed a short while, though, before he said I was of an age not to need a governess any longer."

"Did she go directly from your service to the school?"

"I believe so. He agreed to let her stay – with no pay, of course – until she found other employment. But..."

"Then I must conclude that the moment he read your letter, he recalled the only woman you seemed to be close to – a woman who had every reason to poke him in the eye if she could – and assumed you were on your way to join her. A very inconvenient memory your Uncle Reginald has."

Elinor shook her head. "It never occurred to me he would remember Miss Bradshaw, or where she went."

"It's just as well you had no time to send a message to inform her of your plans, for now Miss Bradshaw will be quite convincing when she tells Uncle Reginald she has no idea where you are. We must just be careful not to arrive at the school before he gives up."

"But what are we to do? Stay here and let him get well ahead of us before we go on?"

"No, for then we might meet him on his return journey, after he finds no success in Chichester." Gus considered the problem.

"If I can't go to Miss Bradshaw, what can I do?" Her voice trembled just a little. "Please, sir, if you will advise me..."

"I suppose now that your plan has gone up in flames, you expect me to rescue you again."

She looked up at him through her lashes. "You're so very good at it, you see."

Gus felt an odd little quiver deep inside him. Indigestion, no doubt, brought on by the never-ending complications she had created in his life. Why hadn't he simply allowed Feather to throw her out of the house this morning?

Because you suspected she'd be amusing.

Of course, that was when he'd expected to be rid of her within a matter of hours. Now he was well and truly stuck, since going on to Chichester wouldn't be feasible for days. What was he to do with her in the meantime?

Slowly a strategy took shape. There was a place, not too far away – and they might as well be comfortable while they waited. He turned the plan over in his mind and could find no flaw.

"You've thought of something." Relief resounded in her voice. "And you'll keep me safe."

She wasn't asking a question, so he didn't answer – but the little quiver had returned to the pit of his stomach.

From Uncle Reginald, yes. But safe, my dear Elinor, is a relative term...

Chapter 3

Just like that morning at his house on Grosvenor Square, when Lord Rackham made up his mind things began to happen in a hurry. Before Elinor could do more than tease a bit to find out what he was planning, she was back in the curricle and they were on their way – to where, she had no idea, except they were no longer traveling south along the road leading to Chichester.

The afternoon sun was still weak, the road was still wet, and the job horses the ostlers had hitched to the curricle were not nearly as quick-moving and smooth-gaited as Lord Rackham's own bays had been. Driving the new team seemed to be more of a chore as well, for he hadn't spoken more than a few words since they had left the inn.

"Augustus," she said finally.

He winced. "It's Rake. Or Gus. Take your choice."

"*Gus* is much better, you know. I observe we are now driving west."

"Very good. You are a country girl after all."

"I'm bad at geography, not directions – at least when I can see the sun. Where are we going? And why did you leave your groom and your own horses at the inn?"

"Jenkins will take the bays back to London. The roads we'll be traveling on now are not as good, and I dislike risking a good team on uncertain terrain."

"Then you don't know the land around here?"

"If you're wondering whether I have a destination in mind, rest assured I do."

Elinor had to admit to feeling a bit easier, knowing they weren't randomly striking off across country.

"And I know the countryside. My yacht is moored

at Portsmouth, so I come this way regularly. Have no fear we will be lost."

His tone was so casual that it took Elinor a moment to register what he'd said. "You have a yacht? No wonder you offered to take Delia abroad – it must be so much easier with your own vessel. I suppose you're quite incredibly rich."

"That is not a comment one makes to a gentleman, brat – but yes, I have enough for my needs."

"Only someone who has never been penniless would phrase it that way, I suspect. What is your yacht like? Is that where you're taking me, only by some roundabout road?"

"Why? Have you changed your mind about wanting to go to Italy with me? – though I'm still not inviting you."

"Of course I haven't. But you told me that Portsmouth lies beyond Chichester. It stands to reason that once we reach Portsmouth, we could approach Miss Bradshaw's school from a different direction and not run the risk of encountering Uncle Reginald."

"Or else we'd run headlong into him in her sitting room. He'll be some time in his travels, I suspect, if he intends to check every inn along the way."

"Every single one? So it wasn't pure chance that he found us? I wonder..."

"What is rolling around in that pretty head of yours, Elinor?"

"I wonder why he put himself to so much trouble," she said slowly, and only then she considered what he had said. Surely calling her *pretty* was only a careless comment. It must be his habit to flatter any woman in his company.

"You are his ward."

"But he was trying so hard to rid himself of me. I don't see why he would go to such effort. You didn't answer, Gus. Is Portsmouth our destination?"

"It is not. I am taking you to a friend's hunting box, which lies a matter of twenty miles from here. Another new adventure for you, I presume, since somehow I doubt either Uncle Reginald or Mr. Dorrance owns such a thing."

Elinor supposed she should mind that he was laughing at her. *I'll think about it later.* "I've heard of such things, of course." She sent a sidelong look at him. "As a matter of fact, the book you loaned me warns of the dangers of trusting gentlemen when they speak of such things as hunting boxes. When you interrupted me this morning, the heroine was about to lose her virtue to such a man."

"I had no idea my library featured such literature. The volume must have been left behind by some random visitor."

"Your sister, perhaps? Your mother? Or do you have cousins or aunts?"

The road ahead of them was empty, but he gazed straight ahead as intently as when he'd threaded their way through the busy streets of London. "Perhaps it was one of my many mistresses."

Elinor shook her head. "You wouldn't bring a mistress into your own home. And even if you did, she wouldn't rely on a book for entertainment."

He gave a bark of laughter. "You are nothing if not original, Elinor. Most young ladies would have fallen into a fit of the vapors if I said anything of the sort to them."

"If you make a habit of sending young ladies to the smelling salts whenever you go into polite society, perhaps it's as well you don't do it often. You've told me nothing about your family, you know. *Do* you have sisters, aunts, cousins?"

"None who matter. You are not concerned that –

like the heroine of your book – you'll find your virtue in danger?"

She supposed she should be worried. Even though he'd been almost a perfect gentleman until now, there had always been people nearby – his servants, or the innkeeper and other guests of the inn. But at an isolated hunting box, things would be different. If they were to be entirely alone...

Her stomach gave an odd little flutter. Fear, she assumed. But that was ridiculous, for she had no reason to be afraid. If Delia was an example of the kind of woman who appealed to Lord Rake, then he would find Elinor just about as attractive as a gatepost. The flutter subsided, but it left behind a kind of flat resignation that confused her, until she concluded it was only relief she was feeling.

"Not at all, for you have no designs on me." Was that a tiny smile playing around the corner of his mouth? Her breath came a little faster. "How long do you think it will be before we dare go on to Chichester? And once at the hunting box, will it be possible for me to send a message to Miss Bradshaw to expect me?"

"It would be possible, I suppose – but hardly wise."

"I expected by the time the news could spread I would already be safe with her. I should hate for her to hear gossip and think the worst of me."

"She'd be a very well-connected schoolteacher if that sort of talk comes readily to her ears."

Gus was correct, of course. There was little danger that London rumor would spread so quickly across the countryside. The fact an obscure young woman had run away from her guardian was hardly the sort of thing a lady of the *ton* would write to a daughter young enough to still be at boarding school. And it was doubtful that anyone Miss Bradshaw corresponded with in the city would be in a position to know the details.

But the notion of sending a message nagged at Elinor nonetheless. It felt important somehow to announce her intentions. But if she could not do so, then she must hope that soon she would be able to stand face to face with her old governess and explain her circumstances.

In the meantime, surely a gentleman's hunting box would offer a reasonable degree of comfort. She might as well enjoy the last few days before she had to leave Gus and settle into an entirely different life.

She frowned. She should be looking forward to this new start, impatient to get on with it – not feeling reluctant to give up this odd accidental companionship.

It's only because I don't know what to expect. She'd come all this way on the assumption there would be some sort of position for her at the school, but it was almost certain her duties would not be glamorous. She might be asked to do anything from tutoring students to scrubbing floors and emptying chamber pots. But no matter what was asked of her, she would be glad to have shelter and food and any honest employment at all.

Even if the very idea made her feel a bit hollow.

* * *

Only half an hour into their drive, his companion had gone oddly quiet. Elinor hadn't asked a single question in a dozen miles, and whenever Gus tried to draw her out, she answered almost at random. He shouldn't be surprised, he supposed, for even a naive and inexperienced girl must have finally comprehended the enormity of what she was doing.

Of course, the situation was a great deal different this afternoon than she had planned. It had been bad enough to spend an entire day in his company. Crossing a good chunk of England in a gentleman's curricle was a racy thing for a young lady to do, but that could be forgiven if he'd been able to deliver her into Miss Bradshaw's care before nightfall. With her safely tucked away under her governess's wing, the talk and the suspicions would be dismissed. With her gone from London, gossip would soon subside. Even Lady Stone's tale of having witnessed a scandalous kiss could be discounted. The old woman was probably a bit short-sighted, after all.

But for a young lady to disappear for a few days somewhere between London and Chichester while in the company of a gentleman, and without a chaperone or even a maid to lend her countenance...

Even the most trusting and innocent of females must realize how close she was sailing to complete ruination. Even the most loyal of former governesses must be suspicious that her charge might not be as blameless as she would like to think. And if the parents of the young ladies who attended Miss Bradshaw's school heard of her antics, then Elinor's hopes of joining the staff in any capacity at all would be smothered before she ever reached Chichester.

A tinge of guilt feathered along his nerves. He ought not to have kissed her, and especially not where Lady Stone could see. He ought not to have carried her off alone. If he'd had any idea their trip would draw out for days, not a mere few hours...

I'd have done it anyway.

He'd been kissed much more expertly, and he'd been kissed with more enthusiasm. But none of those kisses had reached down inside him and clenched his gut in the way Elinor's tentative response had done. What was there about this woman, anyway?

Unless she spent the rest of her life locked away like a nun in a girls' school – a plan that seemed increasingly unlikely with each passing hour – some man would eventually teach her about passion. If she were fortunate, that man would be her husband, and he would be skillful. But if she was unlucky, the man who shared her bed would be crude and selfish, using and discarding her.

Seducing her would be a kindness.

Gus could teach her to enjoy herself in a man's bed. He could teach her how to choose and please a lover. If she was to spend her life as a mistress – and that might well be the only option left to her, after this escapade – he could at least make life more pleasant for her.

Her lessons would take time, of course, but as it turned out, Gus was in no hurry. And afterward – when he tired of her, as he always did tire of the women who came and went in his life – he would make certain her next protector would cherish her and treat her well.

He almost missed the turnoff to Gerald's hunting box because he was contemplating how long it might take to woo her into his bed and then to teach her everything she would need to know. But the job horses were tired and lacking spirit, so he was able to haul them up short and swing the curricle into the long lane.

The sudden turn seemed to rouse Elinor from her reverie, and she sat up straighter and peered ahead down the twin rows of oak trees lining the approach to the miniature manor house half a mile from the road. "*That's* a hunting box?"

"It's what my friend calls it. What did you expect?"

"Something more like a cottage, I suppose. I thought it a place where a few gentlemen retreated to hunt, or to gamble, or to...." She colored a little.

He'd like to pursue that last idea and find out exactly what she was thinking – maybe even get a demonstration. But there would be plenty of time when his hands weren't occupied with reins. "Even if their main activity is tramping across country in the wet and cold while stalking game, gentlemen generally prefer to have creature comforts waiting on their return. Hot food, ample drinks, warm beds – all requiring servants. And even gentlemen who enjoy each others' company a great deal also like to be private at times."

The pink flush in her cheeks intensified.

Was it the suggestion of warm beds that had made her blush? Gus wondered how far the delicate heat spread across her body. Down her throat, certainly. Would her breasts go warm with embarrassment as well?

He couldn't wait to find out.

* * *

The house wasn't the largest Elinor had ever seen. But the sun-warmed brick manor at the end of a long lane lined by tall oaks was certainly one of the prettiest. It sat low to the ground, nestling into a hillside, just two full stories topped by a row of dormer windows marking what was most likely servants' quarters. A pair of symmetrical wings curved out from the main entrance, and dark slate on the roof contrasted nicely with the caramel-colored brick. A stable block stood off to one side, with what looked like an orchard on the other, the fruit trees blooming in the April sun.

The curricle crunched to a halt on the gravel drive by the front door, and a boy came running from the stables. As soon as the stable boy had control of the exhausted horses, Gus climbed down and turned to help Elinor.

The front door swung open and a gaunt-faced servant stared at them. "Lord Rackham!" His gaze slid on to take stock of Elinor, and his voice dropped. "This is a surprise, my lord. You should know things have changed here at Candle Lodge after Lord Burnside's marriage."

Gus said briskly, "When a man gets himself leg-shackled, many things change. But I trust the custom of offering hospitality to Lord Burnside's intimates continues."

"It does, sir," the butler said stiffly, "though Mrs. Pollack may not exactly approve of..."

"Mrs. *who?*" Gus ushered Elinor across the threshold and, smiling down at her, pushed back the hood of her cloak. The ring he wore on his smallest finger caught in her hair and a lock came loose, tumbling down the side of her face. His fingertips brushed her throat – accidentally, of course; there was no reason why she should feel as though his touch lingered, threatening to scorch her skin.

"Mrs. Pollack, sir. The new housekeeper," the butler murmured. "The first thing Lady Burnside did was to turn off the previous one."

"That's inconvenient," Gus said.

A footman coughed suggestively. Biggs turned to look over his shoulder and raised his voice. "Mrs. Pollack, this is Lord Burnside's friend, the Earl of Rackham, and his.... I believe you said the young lady is your cousin, sir?"

"*Cousin?*" The housekeeper sniffed. "I'll believe that one when there are seven Sundays in a month, Biggs. I know quite well the sort of female who visited Candle Lodge while my predecessor was in charge of the household, and I won't stand for that sort of behavior starting up again."

Gus's mouth twisted into a painful-looking grimace, and his fingers tightened on the gold toggles at the neckline of Elinor's cloak.

For a moment she wondered if he actually meant to choke her – until she realized the tightness in her throat had an entirely different cause. *Cousin* must be a euphemism she'd never heard before for *mistress*.

It had been one thing to think logically and objectively about the consequences of deliberately ruining her reputation, when she'd been safely in London and the entire thing was an intellectual exercise. It was something else to actually face contempt – and from a servant at that.

Gus turned to face the woman and said levelly, "Mrs. Pollack, is it?"

"Yes, sir. I'm in charge here in Lady Burnside's absence, and I follow her wishes. If your lordship has indeed brought a member of the muslin company to Candle Lodge, I'll thank you to take her elsewhere." The irate housekeeper's gaze slid past him and came to rest on Elinor.

I must look a fright. Despite the efforts of the maid at the Blue Boar, Elinor's cloak still showed mud spatters from the morning's rain. Her hair was falling down, and she was so tired she could barely stand. But Elinor hadn't managed Uncle Reginald's home and his staff for nothing.

"Mrs. Pollack," she said firmly. "If I were actually a doxy, I would scarcely allow myself to look like a bedraggled mongrel. While I applaud your desire to keep the moral tone of the household high, I've had a very long and difficult day, and right now, I'd prefer to be offered a cup of tea rather than a sermon."

The woman's eyes widened and her voice was little more than a squeak. "Oh. Of course, ma'am. Miss. My lady."

Gus was staring at her, his jaw slack. Elinor considered telling him to close his mouth. "*Miss Elinor* will do, Mrs. Pollack."

"Yes, Miss Elinor. I do beg your pardon, miss, for thinking you ... I mean ... of course you're a young lady.

But Lord Rackham has a reputation... I mean... I've heard tales..."

"As have I, though I do not foresee a time when I will wish to compare notes with you on the matter. Now – the tea?"

The housekeeper gulped, made her curtsy, and hurried away toward a green baize door under the curving staircase.

Biggs goggled at Elinor, who shed her cloak and handed it to him. He almost dropped it. "The drawing room must be this way?" she guessed, and Biggs nodded and swallowed hard. "Perhaps you will accompany me, Cousin. I'm certain Biggs will be able to find something suitable to cut the dust that seems to be coating your throat and keeping you from speaking up."

Gus followed her into the drawing room. "Where did you learn to do that? The tone of voice, the way you brought her to heel..."

"I was just sixteen when I took over the management of Uncle Reginald's household. I had to make it plain who was in charge, or the servants would have run over me."

"Let me guess. When Uncle Reginald decided you were too old for a governess, he fired his housekeeper as well? You sent shivers down my neck, you know."

"Well-deserved ones, I should say. Did you really bring..." Elinor thought better of the question hovering on her tongue. She probably didn't want to know how many women he had brought to Candle Lodge, or how often he had been a guest here, or how long he and his companions had stayed on each visit.

If she was being honest, however, she had to admit feeling more than a bit of curiosity about who those women had been. Were they only ladybirds, as Mrs. Pollack so clearly believed? Or was Elinor closer to the mark in suspecting that those women had been ladies? –

by birth at least, if not in behavior. Would Delia have been one of them eventually, if Gus had had his way?

Perhaps she still will be. Not at Candle Lodge, of course; Mrs. Pollack had made that painfully clear. But there must be other cozy nests that didn't include a dragon like the inimitable housekeeper.

By now, the most notorious gossip in London must have whispered the news about Gus's new companion into Delia's ear. But what would the beauty do?

Gus moved from the fireplace where he'd been standing with his back to the flames to sit next to Elinor on an overstuffed settee. "You're frowning," he said softly. He turned her toward him and cupped her face in his hands. His thumbs rested against the crease between her brows. "What is disturbing you, my dear?"

I'm foolish enough to hope you don't get what you want. The admission startled her, for why should she care? "I was just wondering," she said almost at random. "If Delia reconsiders her decision, how will she let you know she wants you to come back?"

"*If?*" The warm pads of his thumbs slid slowly outward toward her temples, tugging at the crease in her forehead until it smoothed.

Elinor fought the urge to lean into his hands. "How will she even know you're still within reach? You might already be on the open seas."

"You didn't sound so doubtful when you proposed this plan."

Each long, strong, rhythmic stroke of his thumbs made her breath hitch in her throat. "Now that our plans have changed, she'll have even less of an idea where to find you."

"Very true."

"Doesn't it bother you?"

"That our plans have changed? Not at all, Elinor."

"I meant, doesn't it bother you that she won't know

where to send a message?" His fingertips pressed lightly against her face, and though there was no force in the way he held her, Elinor found herself unable to move. "Stop it, Gus," she whispered. "You don't want to do this."

He moved closer. She could feel the warmth of his lips despite the space that remained between his mouth and hers. "Oh, but I do want to."

"It must be this place," Elinor said desperately. "If you've always come here with a mistress, you have no idea how to behave without one."

He was close enough to share her breath now, and her body alternately shivered and trembled.

A tap sounded on the drawing room door, and Gus drew away without hurry. "Come," he called.

To Elinor's surprise, she didn't feel relieved; instead something very like disappointment washed over her. *What is wrong with you?* "I'm surprised Lady Burnside replaced only the housekeeper, for it's plain from his actions the butler was a willing participant in the goings-on."

"The butler answers to the master of the house. And Biggs is very loyal to his master."

The tray Biggs set before her was almost a duplicate of the one Gus's butler had brought into his library – could it possibly be only hours since she had sipped at her tea and argued her case? Elinor felt as if weeks had passed since then.

She filled her cup and watched idly as Gus poured what smelled like brandy.

Biggs stood at attention. "My lord, Mrs. Pollack requested me to inquire how long you and Miss Elinor will be staying."

"No more than a few days."

"Very good, sir. I shall inform her. Your rooms will be ready very shortly."

Elinor's hand clenched on her cup for a moment before she forced herself to relax and smile. What sheer foolishness to worry about those rooms being adjoining ones, or part of the same suite. In truth, she had nothing to fret about, so long as Mrs. Pollack was in charge.

* * *

After her cup of tea, Elinor went upstairs, guided by a still-chastened Mrs. Pollack, and found herself in a surprisingly elegant bedroom overlooking the gardens at the back of the house. The bed posts stretched almost to the ceiling with blue velvet hangings draping the frame, and a fire burned cheerfully in the hearth.

She looked around approvingly and decided it was time to throw the housekeeper a bone. "You do a very nice job of keeping up the house, Mrs. Pollack."

"Thank you, miss. I do my best. Lord Rackham will be in the far wing, and since your own maid has been delayed on the road, Betsy here will wait on you. She's not a lady's maid, but she has nimble fingers and is very willing to learn."

The girl she indicated bobbed a curtsy and went back to unpacking the crumpled garments from Elinor's bandbox.

"If there is anything you need, please ring for me or let Betsy know. Dinner will be served at eight."

Elinor was fairly certain dinner would not be a consideration; she suspected if she once sat down in a chair which was actually comfortable, she might not wake until morning. It would be just as well, too, if she saw as little as possible of Gus. In a house like this one, each of them could surely find plenty of individual entertainment. The little interlude in the drawing room would not be repeated. And if a tiny part of her felt regret at that knowledge – well, the wiser portion of her would eventually win out.

Betsy closed the door behind Mrs. Pollack, and her broad, freckled face creased in a grin as she turned to Elinor. "Thank you, my lady."

"I'm not *my lady*, Betsy, and what are you thanking me for? Surely I've only added to your duties."

"I've always wanted to try my hand at taking care of the ladies."

"I should think, working at Candle Lodge, you'd have had plenty of opportunities."

"Oh, I just came here a few months ago, after Lord Burnside was married. My mum said it wasn't a fit place to work before."

Elinor had no answer.

"But Lady Burnside brings her own lady's maid, and you're the first guest to stay here since I started to work. It's just lucky for me that you were separated from your maid, to give me this chance. Mrs. Pollack says you'll probably want a nap and I should turn down the coverlet and help you undress so you don't crumple your gown."

Elinor didn't want to bother, but she supposed Betsy was right, since she had only two dresses to her name. And she had to admit stretching out between cool, smooth sheets on a plump and well-aired mattress felt far better dozing in a chair.

Betsy drew the sheet up over her and rattled on cheerfully as she bustled around the room. "What a shame at least one of your trunks didn't arrive with you. But I'll do my best."

That was the last Elinor heard.

She woke slowly, feeling as if she'd been dragged up from the bottom of a very deep, dark well. Though the room was dim and the curtains drawn, the light of the lamp Betsy held as she leaned over the bed seemed uncomfortably bright.

The maid looked worried. "I thought you were *never* going to wake, ma'am. I've been trying for ever so long to rouse you – and now you barely have time to dress."

"Dress? For what?"

"Dinner, miss. Lord Rackham said he'd come to escort you down."

Lord Rackham said? Elinor wondered when he'd found time for a conversation with the maid. She could ask for a tray to be brought to her room instead. But she and Gus had already been trouble enough – arriving without notice, needing rooms and tea and dinner, taking servants away from their usual duties...

Betsy was holding up a dark green dinner dress, cut in the latest style, with lace flounces along the hem and a neckline so low it was scandalous.

"What do you think of this?" she asked eagerly.

"I think it is not mine."

Betsy beamed. "I slipped into the mistress's room and borrowed it. You being a lady and all, I expect if Lady Burnside were here she'd be happy to loan you a gown."

Only if Elinor was her own guest rather than an accidental intruder. But in any case, she would not take the chance of spilling soup on Lady Burnside's dark green silk.

"I am certain my own gown will do as well," she said firmly.

Gus could hardly expect elegance when he knew very well she had nothing suitable to wear. And why did the idea of elegance even occur to her? Surely she was wiser than to try to impress Lord Rake!

Betsy looked disappointed, but she helped Elinor into the plain blue gown the mantua-maker had supplied. It really did fit well, and Elinor congratulated herself on the good luck of finding it already made.

As she scooped her hair up in a simple knot at the back of her head, Elinor tried to ignore the maid's muttering. Finally she reminded, "You said yourself there isn't time tonight to do anything fancy, Betsy."

"Do you mean tomorrow you'll let me try out some ideas?" the maid asked eagerly. "And you'll use Lady Burnside's shawl at least, won't you? Your dress is so very plain."

A tap on the door distracted Elinor, and Betsy draped the shawl in place, then ran to open it. Gus, in full evening garb, stood outside.

The first glimpse of his elegance made Elinor suck in a deep and painful breath. His black evening coat fit perfectly, showing off broad shoulders and trim waist. His linen was snowy, the cravat perfectly creased and highlighted by a ruby nestled into the folds – the only spot of color he displayed.

Next to him, she felt like a bedraggled bird, despite the neatness and perfect fit of her plain blue dress – and for just an instant she wished she had agreed to wear Lady Burnside's gown.

But it was foolish to think that putting on a fancy gown would make her elegant enough to truly capture his attention.

Gus eyed her from head to foot. "That's a lovely shawl, Elinor."

The only thing he can find to admire about me isn't even my own. "It belongs to our hostess. Perhaps the fact you approve of her taste in such things might eventually help to make you palatable to her, despite your reputation and the bad influence you've been on her husband."

"Why do you assume I was the bad influence? For all you know, Gerald could have been the one who led me astray."

Elinor slanted a look up at him. "I know he's not the one with the naughty nickname."

"There is that, of course," Gus said calmly and offered his arm. "But if you ever heard what the rest of us called him, in our days at Oxford—"

Elinor interrupted hastily. "Betsy, I can manage for myself tonight, so you may go to your own quarters."

The maid shook her head. "Mrs. Pollack would have my head. She gave orders I'm to sleep in the dressing room, just in case you should need me."

More likely the housekeeper's intent was to prevent anyone else in the house from visiting. In fact, should Elinor have reason to climb out of bed in the wee hours of the morning, she wouldn't be surprised to find Mrs. Pollack herself pacing in front of the door as though on guard.

Lord Rackham must have even more of a fearsome reputation with the ladies than Izzy had heard about, if he stood out as legendary even among the many visitors who must have frequented Lord Burnside's hunting box...

As they reached the top of the stairs, Gus said, "I wondered for just a moment there if you were dropping hints. Perhaps even inviting me to come to your room later, when the house is asleep."

"You have quite a vivid imagination, my lord."

"I prefer it when you call me Gus," he said softly.

"But when I do so, you seem to forget proper behavior."

"Oh, no. It's not a matter of which name you use. It's your presence that causes me to forget proper behavior."

"Only because there are no other females close at hand. When it is a man's habit to flirt, he will occupy himself with anyone who is available." Elinor wondered if he would argue the point, and her pulse speeded up a little at the possibility. Would he try to convince her she was different? Did she actually want him to?

"Why, my dear Elinor." He sounded as though she'd said something profound. "In your sheltered life, how did you happen to learn so much about gentlemen?"

"My upbringing involved little of the *ton*, it is true – but I never said I was completely inexperienced. I went to assemblies and parties, and I observed. In any case, that's why I think it best to remain more formal."

"And give Mrs. Pollack reason to question whether you really are my cousin after all."

Elinor couldn't help but notice, however, that he hadn't responded to the charge that he was an unrepentant flirt. *He ignored it because he can't deny it.*

As they crossed the passage to the dining room, Elinor saw the shadowy figure of the housekeeper lurking at the far end of the hall – as though the mention of Mrs. Pollack had summoned her. Elinor intercepted what seemed to be an approving look. She wondered what the woman would have said if Elinor had been wearing Lady Burnside's green silk instead of her own blue dress.

Though she was a bit on edge as they went in to dinner, Gus was on his best behavior throughout the meal, with no suggestive talk and, for a change, no undercurrents of flirtation. He was still outrageous, however – making an extreme statement and then waiting patiently to see what her reaction would be.

Finally, however, Elinor saw the pattern – he *was* still flirting, only with a milder approach. She waited for him to toss out a completely foolish comment about the Tories in Parliament and turned the tables on him with an even more outrageous statement of her own.

Feeling she'd done a great deal to balance the score, Elinor stood up to leave the room just as Biggs swept the cloth from the table and set the port decanter in front of Gus.

He stretched out a hand as if to capture hers. "Stay and have a glass of port with me, Elinor. Or if you prefer something else, I am persuaded Biggs will bring you some ratafia or tea."

For the barest instant, Elinor was tempted. But sanity prevailed, and she smiled and shook her head. "I dare not."

Gus's eyes glittered, and something shivered deep inside her. "Why not? Because I—"

What ridiculous thing was he about to say? *Because I intrigue you? Because you think if you stay you might have second thoughts about refusing me? Because you're afraid I won't try to seduce you?*

Quickly, Elinor cleared her throat and shot a meaningful glance from Gus to the butler.

Gus went on smoothly, "I grant it's unconventional for you to stay – but who will possibly know?"

"Oh, that's not it at all," she murmured. She seemed able to take only shallow breaths, and her voice showed it – suddenly her tone was soft and low. "It's because now I understand you're only arguing to tease me. It wouldn't be fair of me to take advantage of you."

Gus's forehead wrinkled just a little, but he didn't answer.

Lord Rake, without a word to say? Now there was a sight to enjoy! Who among the *ton* would have believed such a thing was even possible?

Elinor gave him her best curtsy and left the room.

Still, much as she enjoyed putting him in his place, she couldn't deny a little tug deep inside her – for part of her longed to stay, to keep talking to him, and to find out what preposterous thing he would say next.

Chapter 4

Even Lord Burnside's best port – and it was very good wine indeed, for Gerald had a notable palate – held no attractions for Gus. He swallowed the first glass almost without noticing the taste, draining it so quickly that Biggs, still supervising the footmen who were carrying out the last of the serving dishes, looked at him askance.

"You're leaving so soon, my lord?" the butler asked delicately.

Gus realized he'd pushed his chair back and started to rise, and thought better of rushing out of the dining room to pursue Elinor. If even Biggs feared he had lost his mind to go chasing after her, then it was clearly a bad idea to do so.

So he settled back in his place at the long table, refilled his glass, and eyed the chair directly across from him, the place where Elinor had dined.

The meal had passed by almost without him noticing the food as they moved from course to course just as smoothly as they had slid from discussing London's attractions to religion to politics.

She had looked adorably prim in the high-necked walking dress – the gown he seemed to have bought for her today in Knightsbridge. Why hadn't he insisted on seeing everything she had selected, so he could add a few more suitable things?

That question had an easy answer, for he'd only taken her to Maria's shop because he'd felt sorry for her – a woman with just one dress to her name was a sad thing indeed. He'd had no idea they'd be spending the evening together, so the need for a dinner gown had never crossed his mind.

By all rights, he should have delivered her to her governess by now and gone on about his business. Most likely, he'd have been well on his way back to London at this hour, even though there were a couple of house parties in the vicinity he'd been invited to join. Perhaps he'd have decided to look in on the entertainment, though he doubted it. The truth was he wouldn't miss the parties at all.

Of course, his reluctance to join in the merrymaking had nothing at all to do with Elinor. Neither of those gatherings had been especially attractive options, certainly not exciting enough to draw him out of the city. The witty, sparkling people he most enjoyed were generally to be found in London at this time of year, not rusticating on their country estates – so he was missing very little by being here instead.

He waited until the servants had all left the dining room and the silence was interrupted only by the small clink of his glass as he set it down on the table between sips and by the occasional crackle of a coal in the fire. It wasn't so much that he was longing to rejoin Elinor, he told himself. If this evening had been like old times, with half a dozen gentlemen occupying Gerald's table, none of them would have been in any particular hurry to rejoin their companions in the drawing room. But drinking port alone was a damned boring pastime.

So why should he punish himself by wasting time with another glass or two? If he was staying only so the butler didn't perceive him to be a fool... well, since when had anything Biggs thought made an impression on the gentlemen he served?

If Gus could find a way around Mrs. Pollack and wear away Elinor's hesitation, he might positively enjoy this little retreat. He'd have fun for a few days, at least – exactly as long as it would take for Cousin Reginald to make his journey all the way to Chichester, give up his mission, and return to London. By the time it would be safe to take Elinor on to her old governess, Gus would no doubt be more than ready to do so.

But right now, he was wasting precious time when he could be engaged in a seduction so gentle that Elinor wouldn't even notice the foundation being cut from under her until she'd fallen into his arms.

Trying to kiss her this afternoon had been decidedly bad judgment, he admitted. He'd stepped forward too boldly, and he'd paid the price. He would have to work carefully to regain lost ground – but regain it he would.

He smiled, pushed back his chair and strode straight across to the drawing room.

But the room wasn't brilliantly lighted as he'd expected, and in the first instant as he stood on the threshold and looked around, he thought she wasn't there. Disappointment trickled through him – though of course it was only because sitting by a drawing room fire by himself wouldn't be any more exciting than drinking port alone had been.

He looked more closely at the single pool of lamplight by the fire, and saw the sweep of a dark blue skirt spilling around the legs of a wing-backed chair. He moved close enough to spot the book she'd taken from his library lying open on Elinor's lap. She looked up as he approached, gave him an absent smile, and turned her attention back to the story.

He sat down on the arm of her chair, turning sideways so he could watch her profile. Her hair smelled like lavender, and it gleamed in the firelight. "You've read quite a lot of your book already."

She turned the page. "I'm finding the story very interesting."

"What's it about?"

She gave a tiny sigh and didn't answer.

"Has the heroine been ruined yet?"

"I suppose I should have expected that would be the part of a love story which would interest you most, Lord Rake."

Gus shrugged. "It's the only event you told me about. What else is happening?"

"More than I could possibly summarize in the short length of time before you would lose interest." She didn't look up.

Clearly this line of conversation was getting him nowhere. Gus moved across to a round table and opened a drawer, pulling out a pack of cards. "Come play piquet with me," he suggested.

"I'm such a poor card player that I would hardly make an interesting opponent."

"I'll teach you."

"Perhaps you hadn't noticed, Gus..." He heard a faint note of irony in her voice. "...but I'm reading. At least I'm trying to."

"Then read to me. I'm sure you have a lovely voice, and it would be good practice for you."

"Practice for what?"

"Reading to the children at Miss Bradshaw's school."

"It's a seminary, Gus, not a school for infants. The *children* are young ladies and old enough to read for themselves."

"Oh." He came back to sit beside her, shuffling the pack of cards. He'd never realized before that the scent of lavender was intoxicating. Or perhaps Gerald's latest shipment of port was much stronger than usual, so only a couple of glasses had left his head swimming.

"It's unlikely I'll be given schoolroom duties, anyway. More probably I'll be cleaning or cooking or running errands." She sounded perfectly calm.

Gus frowned. "You can't mean you actually want

to be a schoolroom drudge."

"What I *want* right now, Gus, is... Oh, never mind. The point is, I'm accustomed to work. I wonder if there might be a sketch book lying about. Or at least a few sheets of paper and a stick of charcoal."

"You're an artist?"

"I am far from being one. But if you insist on talking to me at random intervals so I cannot read, I may as well occupy my hands in other ways."

Other ways. Now there was a good idea.

Gus tossed the pack of cards toward a nearby table and picked up her hand instead. She had set aside her gloves, and her palm lay warm and smooth against his. When she tried to draw away, he held her more firmly, raising her fingers – long, slender, tipped with perfectly-shaped nails – to his lips. A scar along one knuckle caught his attention, and he traced it gently with the edge of his thumbnail. "What accident marred this lovely finger?" he whispered.

She rolled her eyes. "Honestly, Gus, I'd wager you don't even stop flirting when you're asleep."

Would you like to find out?

Before he could ask, she went on. "I was helping my mother pare potatoes, and the knife slipped."

"You haven't said much about your family, other than Uncle Reginald. But he can't be your only relative."

"Actually, he can – and it seems he is. The Holcombe family – such as it is – has frittered itself away until only the two of us are left."

"Then tell me about your parents."

"Why? You can't be interested in a village vicar so unworldly and so poor his wife had only one maid to help with all the work, so she did the cooking herself."

A bit to his surprise, Gus discovered that he was indeed interested. "To be a vicar, your father must have been an educated man."

"His grandfather was a baronet. If you recall, I did warn you we Holcombes are nothing fancy."

Fancy enough to catch my fancy. But a line like that would only set her to rolling her eyes again, and Gus had to admit it was hardly his best work. What was there about the woman that put him off his stride, anyway?

A baronet as great-grandfather, and only one relative in the world. No grand family to be upset about what she did, and – once Uncle Reginald gave up – no one to guard her virtue.

Elinor was the perfect mistress. She was a lady, so she understood the rules – yet she wasn't high enough ranking that taking her into his bed would call down notoriety on a man's head. If he'd designed her himself, Gus couldn't have done a better job.

He turned his attention back to her hand. "And this scar?" He touched a tiny puckered mark on the edge of her hand, between wrist and smallest finger.

"I burned myself while making ginger beer at Uncle Reginald's house in Camberford. He's very fond of ginger beer, so I make gallons each year."

He raised her hand and brushed his lips across the scar. "What will he do without you?"

"Perhaps that's why he was pursuing me. I am said to have a talented hand with ginger beer – though I believe it's only because I got a very good recipe from one of the women in the village. You start with the best Jamaican ginger, you see, and bruise it along with the sugar..."

She sounded as though she was talking at random, and Gus congratulated himself; he was clearly making progress. He gently sucked the very tip of her little finger into his mouth, brushing his tongue against the pad as if accidentally.

She tasted like honey – like one of the sweetmeats they'd been offered after dinner. But he didn't think she'd eaten any of those, so this must just be her – and if her hand tasted so inviting, the rest of her would be like a feast.

He was so aroused he couldn't think clearly.

She shifted in her chair. "Perhaps if you will give me my hand back, I'll reconsider and play cards after all, my lord. Though I cannot imagine you being entertained by the sort of stakes I can afford."

Gus could imagine some very entertaining stakes indeed. His mouth went dry.

While he was distracted she pulled her hand away, slid out of her chair, and stooped to pick up a few cards that had missed the edge of the table and scattered across the carpet. "Perhaps we could ask Mrs. Pollack if she will loan us some pins."

"I doubt she holds with gambling," Gus said. "I'll stake you." He took a twist of paper from a jar on the mantel, held it to the coals, and lit a branch of candles, setting the light to one side of the table.

Elinor looked doubtful. "We could play for the rest of the spills – there are plenty in the jar."

"What fun would that be? I'll play you for a kiss instead."

"Hardly, sir. I've already told you I'm a poor player, so why would I agree to kiss you if I lose?"

"Because you'd like to, I hope. In any case, that wasn't quite what I meant."

Perhaps it was ungentlemanly of him, but he enjoyed watching her struggle. She wanted to ask him to explain; she was curious about the answer, but she suspected that asking the question would only allow him another opportunity for suggestiveness.

She was starting to know him very well, Gus mused.

When it appeared her common-sense side would win – and what a pity that was! – Gus said softly, "If I win, I get to kiss you. If you win, I have to kiss you."

Her face flamed. "In that case, I accept your offer to stake me instead. With money, I mean."

He laughed as he dropped a handful of shillings on the table. "I'm willing to accept a handicap – divide those up with two for you, one for me."

He intended to let her win, but that result required far less finesse than he'd expected. She was just inexperienced enough that her play was hard to predict, and her strategy – such as it was – kept him off balance. He found himself wondering if she'd be just as capricious in bed... and he looked up to find her sweeping the last of his shillings into her own pile.

She stacked the coins neatly and with obvious enjoyment. "Playing cards was far more fun than I expected, Gus."

"I should think it must have been. I would like to meet the person who taught you, for if you believe you're a poor player, your instructor must be a master."

She sobered. "My mother loved cards." She pushed the coins across the table to him. "You were right – it was more fun to play with shillings than with twists of paper."

"Keep your winnings," Gus said softly. "You'll need some pin money."

"But I hazarded nothing."

"Then hang onto that pile until tomorrow, and we'll play again. It will be interesting to see if you play more cautiously when you're risking your own money."

"It won't ever be mine." She gathered up the shillings, tying them into a plain white handkerchief. "You think we'll still be waiting here?"

"I doubt Uncle Reginald can reach Chichester before dusk tomorrow, if he's stopping at every inn along the road. Give him another day for the journey back to London – of course, I'm assuming he takes Miss

Bradshaw's word and doesn't dawdle around Chichester to check up on her. We'll need to stay here until Thursday at least."

"There are many worse places to be, I'm sure."

And many worse people to be with. Gus couldn't think of another woman who wouldn't have driven him mad by now – cooped up together without making love to pass the hours. But he had to admit he was having a surprisingly good time. Playing cards for shillings was hardly his usual pastime, but when his opponent was Elinor...

She had accepted their plight with startlingly good cheer. True, her destination was hardly going to be an Eden, so perhaps a few peaceful days of pleasant surroundings, attentive servants, and no ginger beer to make seemed like paradise to her.

"I'll walk you up to your bedroom," he offered, and was startled when she didn't argue.

But a moment later she let go his arm and turned back. "My book," she explained, snatching it up from the cushion of the wing-backed chair. "Uncle Reginald thinks it a dangerous and wasteful pastime to use up candles in such a way, but I love reading in bed."

In his mind, Gus could see her, curled up amongst the pillows. Candlelight glowing against her warm skin. Her hair tumbling around her shoulders, caressing her throat, curving around a pink-tipped breast... He wasn't certain why she'd be naked if her attention was focused on a book. But as long as it was his daydream, he'd picture her any way he wanted to – including letting those long, slim fingers of hers caress not the gilded leather binding of a book but his own skin... His body would have stirred to life at the mere notion, except he was already so aroused that sanity seemed to have fled altogether.

They were at her bedroom door before he regained

even a measure of common sense. "Good night," she whispered, and the tiny shake of her head – as though she were throwing back a mass of loose hair – instantly burned through his control once more. He reached for her, half-intending to seek out and remove her hairpins just so he could see that glorious mass in its natural state.

She took a step back and the door creaked a little as it opened behind her. For just an instant, Gus wondered if she was issuing an invitation – but an unmistakable snore cut through the silence that separated them. The maid, asleep in the dressing room as ordered.

Ruefully, he returned to sanity – though he wondered if he really would have pressed Elinor to allow him to come in, to share her bed. Surely he would have been wiser than that. Push for too much, too quickly, and she'd have run like a frightened rabbit.

He cleared his throat. "Do you ride? Gerald – Lord Burnside – generally leaves a couple of hunters here."

She looked gleeful, but a moment later she wrinkled her nose. "I've nothing to wear, I'm afraid."

"Of course. I didn't think." He didn't move. "Do you know, Elinor, I really believe I have to kiss you anyway."

She opened her mouth – intending to protest, he was certain, but his body took her small movement as concession. He wanted to swoop down to capture her, to taste her, to drink in the glorious honeyed taste of her. Instead, he took his time, letting his mouth slowly drift toward hers, watching as her lips trembled, as she leaned just the tiniest bit toward him...

He knew he couldn't kiss her properly and then turn away. If he tasted her at all tonight, he would insist on more. So at the last instant, he brushed his lips along the hollow of her cheek instead. Even the touch of satin skin against his mouth set his blood ablaze, and the startled look she gave him – as if amazed he had asked so little of her – almost made him toss long-term strategy to the wind and drag her off to his bedroom after all.

But coercion never paid. If he could apply patient persuasion instead, she would end up in his bed – eventually. The question was whether it would be soon enough for Gus to keep his sanity.

* * *

As Elinor approached the breakfast room, the sound of voices stopped her. One belonged to Gus, of course; surprised though she was to find he was already up at this hour, she could hardly fail to recognize his baritone.

But the other was feminine. Had some woman arrived overnight? Some friend of the Burnsides?

Or perhaps it was some friend of Gus's – a lady, no doubt, if he'd managed to convince Mrs. Pollack that she was to be treated as a regular guest and invited to partake of breakfast.

Embarrassed heat flashed over Elinor. She had actually dreamed about the man last night, imagining he hadn't stopped with kissing her cheek – though soon after that bit of her dream, things had gotten a bit fuddled. Probably because she had no real idea what ought to have happened next...

And that is enough of that. What occurred in her dreams was not within her control, but she could certainly keep her thoughts in line while she was awake.

She found it all too obvious that she hadn't featured in Gus's dreams last night. How perfectly foolish she was, to think a rake of his caliber could be intrigued by someone like her. He had simply been bored enough to flirt, until this woman – whoever she might be – had arrived.

Elinor told herself she was delighted to have some

warning, so she didn't bounce into the breakfast room like a puppy eager to play. She would politely say good morning, and then she would mind her own business for the rest of the day and let Gus and his friend go about theirs.

But first, she'd get a very good look at the woman Gus found more appealing.

She was startled to find that the woman in the breakfast room was the housekeeper, standing near the head of the table with her hands folded, perfectly still. Elinor felt like a fool. Not even Gus would be able to sneak a lady-love past Mrs. Pollack's watchful gaze; what was wrong with her that she had leaped to such a conclusion?

"I appreciate it, Mrs. Pollack, and I know my cousin will too." Gus stood as Elinor came in. "Mrs. Pollack will search out a habit for you so we can ride this morning."

The housekeeper nodded and went out.

So we can ride, he had said. Elinor would have another morning in his company... as well as in the sunshine and fresh air, of course. The freedom of being on horseback – and not the fact that she'd have Lord Rake's attention for another half-day – must be why she was suddenly feeling so very pleased with the world.

* * *

The riding habit Mrs. Pollack had found stashed in a wardrobe somewhere wasn't the best color for Elinor; Gus would have dressed her in russet if the choice had been his, to bring out the shades of red and gold in her hair. Also, though it fitted reasonably well, the garment's previous owner had been a bit less well-endowed. Gus found his gaze drifting over the rows of military-style braid that marched down the bodice, wondering if the breasts beneath the fabric were really as lush and bountiful as his imagination pictured.

The geldings in Gerald's stable had easy gaits and pleasant temperaments, and Elinor was a good rider, so he soon relaxed and began to enjoy the outing. They flushed a covey of quail, and stopped by an almost-hidden pond to watch a duck and her flock of babies swimming in aimless circles.

"I suppose you're judging how soon they'll be full grown and ready to hunt," Elinor said.

Gus shrugged. "It's a pleasant pastime to tramp across the fields with a shotgun and a dog or two. And one must eat. Are you hungry, by the way?"

"Yes, and I suppose you mean it's time to head back." She sounded almost sad.

"Not exactly. There's a shady spot up ahead, under that tree." He led the way, swinging out of his saddle to help her down before he tethered the horses where they could graze.

From one saddlebag he extracted a small blanket and spread it out on the grass. From the other he took provisions – fresh bread, cheese, apples, and a bottle of wine.

"How did you manage to wheedle a picnic out of Mrs. Pollack?"

Expertly, he pulled the cork. "I went straight to the source. I've known Cook a long time."

"Oh. You mean she was here when..." Elinor's voice trailed off, but Gus could almost hear her mind working. *When this place was the site of debauchery.*

He wanted to say it hadn't been like that. So far as Gus knew, nothing had ever happened at the hunting box that hadn't been approved by all parties involved... so there was no need for him to feel defensive now. And why should he care what she believed, or whether she had the facts right? In another few days, she would be gone from his life.

Unless I decide to keep her...

He dismissed the thought as a random aberration. "Gerald and I have been friends since we were boys. Cook used to be in charge of the kitchens at his family estate, before she decided she wanted an easier life and came here."

"An easier life? Taking care of..." She sighed. "Sorry. I shouldn't have mentioned it."

He wondered, as he poured wine into a cup for her, what she had imagined – and whether she'd be willing to make those fantasies real.

Probably not. Regretfully, he turned his attention to slicing bread and cheese.

"This is really lovely, Gus." She leaned back against the tree trunk, and Gus almost cut himself because he was watching to make certain her habit didn't split.

No, he admitted. He was watching to make certain if it *did* split, he wouldn't miss the view. But the fabric held and he returned reluctantly to his task.

"And I shouldn't have said anything about... Well, whatever has happened here in the past, it's not my affair."

Pity, that.

"Quite true." He passed her a slice of bread and cheese. "Not the most elegant of meals."

"But it's very good, nevertheless. The fresh air has given me an appetite." She laughed. "I wonder what Izzy would say, if she could see me now – picnicking under a tree with Lord Rake."

"Who's Izzy? No, wait – don't tell me. Lady Stone said something about her. Arlington's brat?"

"You have an excellent memory, my lord."

"I do when young ladies are concerned – especially the ramshackle ones who are never slow to take up a challenge."

"That's Izzy. She would have held out for Paris, by the way."

He sliced an apple and handed her a chunk. "And you? Does Paris hold no attraction for you?"

"What point is there in wishing? My future lies in a different direction."

"It doesn't need to," he said softly.

She stared at him, her forehead wrinkled. "I don't know what you mean."

"You can't really believe that after this escapade – announcing you were running off with a man, leaving London with a known rake, spending days alone with me – you can just go on to Miss Bradshaw's school and pretend none of it happened."

"I have no other option but the school."

"There are always options, Elinor." He cleared his throat. "There are gentlemen who would welcome your companionship."

Her gaze was earnest. "As a mistress, you mean."

She sounded quite calm about it, and Gus's pulse leaped. If she'd already accepted the reality, then it was just one more very small step to welcoming him as her lover.

But she stood up abruptly, her movements jerky. The bread and cheese tumbled from her lap to the blanket. "I'll be going back to the house now. If you would do me the favor of helping me back into the saddle—"

What the hell just happened? He leaped to his feet. "Of course I'll help you, but—"

"Then I'll leave you to finish your lunch and your ride."

"Elinor, you're not riding off by yourself and leaving me here."

"Afraid to be left alone, are you?" The corners of

her mouth turned up as if by reflex, but the expression in her eyes held not only anger but loss, hurt, and shame. She quickly looked away and busied herself with gathering up the remains of their picnic.

She feels shamed. What a nodcock he was, to be so clumsy.

He went to bring the horses, steadying her gelding. She had to stand very close so he could help her mount, and the scent of lavender drifted around him and made his head swim.

She couldn't ride away without his help; she had to stay there and listen – so before he bent to help her into the saddle, he said, "Why did you assume I meant *affaires*, anyway?"

When she finally answered, her voice dripped sarcasm. "Oh, it might have been the fact you referred to gentlemen in the plural."

Gus frowned. "I could have been speaking of the companionship of marriage."

"*You*, Lord Rake? Actually suggesting that any gentleman contemplate marriage? What a surprise that would be."

Gus was disgruntled. "I never said I was against the institution altogether. I suppose eventually even I will have to–" What was wrong with him? He certainly wasn't going to discuss his own situation with this chit. "To be perfectly clear, I didn't mean me!"

"There is no need to reassure me on that score, sir. And even if you should be addled enough to offer marriage, I would refuse you without a second thought." She put her foot into his clasped hands with – he noticed – far more force than was necessary to get her up into the saddle. She started off toward the house without waiting for him to repack the saddlebags and mount his own gelding.

He kept her in sight throughout the ride back, but

only by pressing his mount. By the time he left the gelding in the stable, a stable boy was already grooming her horse and Elinor was gone.

* * *

Tears threatened on the ride and spilled over the moment Elinor left her horse with the stable boys and turned toward the house. She didn't know if she was feeling insulted or angry, but a good part of her wished she'd slapped Gus's face before she left him.

How dare he speak so calmly about her becoming a mistress, as though it were a job like any other? Because that *was* what he'd been talking of; the mention of marriage had been only an afterthought, a feeble attempt to deflect her fury.

But she had to admit that mostly she was angry because he was right – about being a mistress, not about the possibility of marriage. Gentlemen did not actually marry girls like Elinor. They chose girls like Izzy Arlington. Izzy was a minx to be sure, but she was a fascinating and unpredictable and, most importantly, a wealthy and well-connected one.

Gus had made it clear that Elinor – who had neither a truly noble name nor the sizable dowry that would overcome the lack of a pedigree – was suitable only to be a mistress. She could run a gentleman's home, entertain his friends, satisfy him in bed, perhaps even bear him a child. All the duties of a wife, but without the honor of carrying his name.

How dare he imply I would find such an arrangement acceptable?

And yet... Was he right in thinking that she could not now go on to Chichester and win a spot at Miss Bradshaw's school? In her eagerness to escape Mr. Dorrance, had she ended by destroying herself?

She was halfway across the courtyard when a footman came around the front corner of the house, leading an exhausted, lathered horse. Someone, Elinor deduced, had been in quite a hurry.

With her eyes still stinging from tears she would just as soon the servants didn't see, she ducked her head and went in a side entrance. Raised voices echoed through the entrance hall. Perhaps the uproar drew her attention because any distraction would be welcome. Or maybe she recognized the signs because she had so recently been involved in just such a standoff herself, when she had tried to enter Gus's house on Grosvenor Square.

She paused in the shadow of the stairway to listen. Was that – could it be – Uncle Reginald shouting? She held her breath to listen.

"If you have my young relative secreted here, I shall have the law on you!" he blustered. "All of you! I'm a justice of the peace myself, and I know my rights!"

Yes, that was Uncle Reginald – but how was it possible he was here?

Her position must have been more exposed than she realized, for Uncle Reginald pushed past Biggs. "There she is, right there. Elinor, you young fool – come here this minute!"

She shrank away from his outstretched hand, but the wainscoting was at her back; there was no place to run.

Elinor had believed when she left their picnic site that she would as soon never see Gus again – but when the side door banged and he loomed up beside her, relief threatened to swamp her. Gus would make everything right. *He always does.*

He scanned the room and turned to the butler. "What is going on here, Biggs?"

Biggs drew himself up tall. "This … gentleman …

forced his way into the house, my lord. He seems to be searching for your ... young cousin."

Uncle Reginald faced Gus squarely. "*Your* cousin? I think not! You were at the inn. Shady characters there, all of you, though I was quite a way on down the road toward Chichester, thinking she must have run to her old governess, before I realized how suspiciously you'd acted. Did she accost you there?"

"She did not," Gus said calmly.

"Then you must have been the one who brought here there. It doesn't matter now. I've come to take her home, where her affianced husband is waiting."

Elinor found her voice. "You've gone to all this trouble for nothing, Uncle. Mr. Dorrance wouldn't marry me anyway, now I'm ruined."

He laughed scornfully. "You think I was fool enough to tell him about your note and how you sneaked away? So far as he knows, you're in your room suffering from a catarrh."

She hadn't expected him to be so cunning, or so quick-thinking. The disease he had assigned her was threatening enough so no one could visit, but it wasn't a chronic condition – nothing that would make a suitor think twice.

It seemed she had underestimated Uncle Reginald at every turn. He had been quick to pursue, quick to realize her real plan, quick to sense the next move when her scheme had come apart. And he had cut off her last hope by keeping Mr. Dorrance in the dark...

But Uncle Reginald didn't know the full story. There had been that kiss in Grosvenor Square, in front of the most notorious gossip in London – and though it seemed Lady Stone didn't know Reginald Holcombe after all, she had no doubt spread the story far and wide. If the old lady had lived up to her reputation, Elinor would have none left at all... "All of society must know by now that I'm ruined. I'd be no good to Mr. Dorrance."

Uncle Reginald paused for a bare instant, then shook his head. "It doesn't matter. He'll keep his sworn word and live up to the contract he signed, or I'll sue him for breach of promise. If you've lost all your acquaintances in the *ton*, that will be unfortunate for him – and no doubt it'll be a problem for you as well, when he learns it – but it's no concern of mine."

Elinor gasped. "You care so little for me, after all these years, that you would hand me over to a husband who might well beat me?"

Uncle Reginald shrugged. "I'm not the one who ran away from a perfectly-respectable match, Elinor."

Gus stepped forward and said lazily, "Would you care for a brandy, sir?"

Elinor stared at him, aghast. What was wrong with him? How could he listen to her being coerced and threatened, and then offer hospitality to the man who was brutalizing her? She had uttered some sharp words, yes – said things in a way she regretted – but surely that wasn't cause enough for Gus to take Uncle Reginald's side! What had happened to the protector she had come to count on?

And just when – and why – had she begun to put so much faith in Lord Rake that she had lost her own power of reason?

"I care only for taking what I came for," Uncle Reginald grunted. "Come, Elinor – right now."

Lazily, Gus stepped between them. "You can hardly drag her away without allowing her to pack her fripperies. Besides, that's a borrowed riding habit she's wearing – the owner would object if she took it with her. Come along into the study, sir." Without a word or even a bow to Elinor, he ushered Uncle Reginald off as if they were the best of friends.

As if I mean nothing to him. Because I don't.

Truth struck Elinor hard. No wonder he'd tried to steer her into a career as a mistress. Gus was looking forward to being free – not stuck at his friend's hunting box for an indefinite future, with the moralistic Mrs. Pollack watching him every minute. He must be even more relieved to find that Uncle Reginald wasn't issuing demands for Gus himself to step up, marry Elinor, and preserve her honor.

Not that he'd actually do anything of the sort – as he'd made painfully clear – but at least he wouldn't have to fight a duel over the question.

She was truly on her own. She supposed the best she could hope for was that Gus and Uncle Reginald would find so much to chat about that she could get a head start. If she took a horse from the stables and set out toward Chichester right now...

But if she disappeared again, Uncle Reginald would assume she was once more headed toward Miss Bradshaw's school. He'd catch up with her within hours.

She'd have to go somewhere else. She must leave the sanctuary of the hunting box and take an unknown road, with no destination in mind and not a glimmer of an idea about what might lie in her path.

Her heart twisted. *That's because I'm afraid.* Certainly – after what he'd said and what he'd done – she couldn't be feeling regret at the idea of leaving Gus!

Chapter 5

Gus showed Reginald Holcombe into Gerald's little-used study and stepped back out into the passage to summon Biggs. Before Gus could issue orders, the butler nodded. "Of course, my lord. Brandy right away, and a footman to build up the fire so your guest will be comfortable. Will there be anything else?"

"Tell Miss Holcombe to go to her room and stay there. Do that first, before the brandy."

Biggs' forehead wrinkled. "Yes, my lord. Ah – do you think she will comply?"

"Good point. Send the footman out to the stable to tell them Miss Holcombe is not to take a horse out under any circumstances. After that, he can come tend to the fire. I don't really care whether Uncle Reginald is comfortable."

The butler nodded and went off.

Gus closed the door. "I'm curious, sir," he said lightly. "You did say you found my behavior suspicious when you were making inquiries at the Blue Bull. But I wondered how you traced us from there."

"It was hardly difficult, for someone accustomed to dealing with the logic and reasoning that accompanies legal work."

The man makes it sound as if he sits on the King's own bench.

"Once I decided to return to that particular inn, it was no challenge at all to find the ostler who had hitched up the team of job horses that brought you here. Or the one who groomed them, after they were returned by Lord Burnside's man."

Damn, Elinor was right. I should have used my own horses.

"I do beg your pardon, my lord, for not properly introducing myself before. You understand I was reluctant to make your acquaintance at all until I realized you were a man of sense, not the kind to steal a female away. I must say, however, I am surprised at finding Elinor here."

"But not surprised that she stood up to you and ran away?"

"It's true she can display a tendency to be stubborn, but she's always been biddable, in the end."

A tendency to be stubborn? That's like saying the ocean is a bit damp." Gus wondered what sort of treatment Elinor had suffered to make her obey the whims and dictates of this autocrat.

"Indeed. What I find strange is how she managed to draw you – a man of good sense – into her scheme. She was never the sort to appeal to the men, you know."

"Then the men in question were blind and stupid," Gus muttered.

"What did you say, sir? At any rate, I'm simply glad to have found her. Of course, for such a flighty female as she has shown herself to be, marriage is the only answer."

"Even if the lady is unwilling?"

"The lady will come to realize she has no choice." Reginald stretched his feet out to the meager fire. "Your servants aren't worth much, are they? In my house they'd have snapped to attention, or I'd know the reason why. You said something about brandy?"

"I'm certain Biggs is acting on my orders."

"Then you're more patient than I. What was I saying?"

"That Elinor has no choice about taking a husband."

"Well, she doesn't. Marry she must, after this escapade – and marry she shall."

"You would see a girl her age wedded to an old man?"

"Mr. Dorrance is not old, though he might appear so to her."

"Then he is forty? Fifty?"

"Perhaps a little older," Reginald admitted. "I can't see it matters, since he's her only prospect. Unless *you're* willing to marry her, my lord?"

Gus's hand clenched on the back of a chair. He looked down at his knuckles, noticing with detachment that they'd turned white with the pressure of his grip. Better, he supposed, to squeeze a chair than to plant Uncle Reginald the facer he deserved...

What a fool I am.

"I didn't think it likely." Reginald gave a nasty little chuckle. "I'll thank you kindly to keep your nose out of it and leave Elinor's future to me."

Biggs came in quietly with a decanter and two glasses on a tray, with a footman following. He gave Gus the smallest of nods as he poured the brandy.

The footman stirred the fire to life, added a log, and went away.

Gus swirled brandy in his glass and watched his guest. Faced with a scandal, and offered the opportunity to force a marriage between his young cousin and the titled gentleman who had compromised her, why had Reginald Holcombe not demanded that Gus step in and preserve Elinor's honor? Instead, he'd brought up the possibility in such an off-handed way that it was clear he hadn't pondered the idea for more than a moment.

What made an elderly wine merchant such a prize? Why was this marriage so important to Uncle Reginald that he had chased them across England?

Reginald sipped and nodded. "Brandy's not my drink, really, but I'll allow this is fine stuff. My friend Mr. Dorrance is in the business, you know. Wine, spirits, all sorts of drink. If you ever need to restock the cellars..."

"I'll keep him in mind," Gus lied. "Is that what made his offer for Elinor's hand so acceptable to you? Did he agree to keep your wine cellar full? Or was it something else?"

Reginald smiled slyly.

Gus let the brandy barely touch his lips and forced a cajoling note into his voice. "Ah. I thought there must be something you gain from the marriage. Come, Mr. Holcombe – we're both men of the world. You can tell me."

And if you don't speak up, I'll be happy to choke it out of you, you miserable little worm...

* * *

The stable master shook his head. "I'm sorry, miss, but if I was to give you a horse after my lord ordered me not to..."

Elinor felt like stamping her foot. "I suppose you think it would cost you your job? But Lord Rackham is not your employer, so he can't send you away."

"I don't want to find out what he'd do instead." The man sighed. "Much as I'd like to be obliging to you, miss..."

With her shoulders slumped in despair, Elinor walked back toward the house. She could simply stroll off through the gardens and away, she supposed – for all the good it would do her. Freedom of that sort would be short-lived.

She could go to Mrs. Pollack, confess the entire story, and ask for protection. At least the housekeeper, unlike the burly stable master, didn't seem to be afraid of Gus – but she had little power to stand between a guardian and a ward. She'd be no help where Uncle

Reginald was concerned.

Or Elinor could barricade herself in her room and refuse to come out. She wondered how long it would be before someone broke the door down. Gus, probably – because if she pulled off such a dramatic performance, he'd be even more eager to see the last of her. No doubt he'd given the order about horses because such a feeble attempt at flight would only delay the inevitable, and he'd rather be done with her right now.

But even if Uncle Reginald took her back to London, Elinor might still be able to escape without marrying Mr. Dorrance. She could tell him what she'd done, and hope he would back out after all. But she suspected Uncle Reginald would arrange it so the next time she laid eyes on the wine merchant would be at the altar with the marriage ceremony already in progress.

If she could slip away from the house in Bloomsbury once more – but even if she could manage to do so with all the eyes that would be on her, where would she go? Izzy was in no position to help; she was probably in enough trouble herself after their escapade at Vauxhall – and how long ago *that* seemed!

Delia. How could she have forgotten about Delia?

Elinor could solve her own problem and Gus's, too. If she admitted to Delia that the gossip was all a scheme for Gus to win her affections, then perhaps the woman would be so relieved – possibly even grateful – that she'd give Elinor the help she needed.

But that was only a mad daydream, born of desperation. Elinor didn't even know the woman's full name, much less where to find her. And as for the idea of throwing herself at the feet of the lady Gus cared about, and pleading his case...Could she really do that?

Not after he'd abandoned her to her fate and cheerfully gone off to entertain Uncle Reginald. Elinor would walk through hot coals barefoot before she'd help him win his lady-love.

She was truly on her own. Worse, she was caught in a trap – and she had to admit she had sprung it on herself. She had been fooling herself all along, thinking she could go to Miss Bradshaw – for if Lady Stone really was the *ton*'s most notorious gossip, then by now Elinor had no reputation left. She couldn't work in a school where impressionable girls were sent; the parents and the school governors would never allow it.

Her options were even more cruelly limited than they had been before she left London – before they had detoured to Candle Lodge. At least Gus had been honest with her about her plight; he hadn't even tried very hard to soften the truth.

As she weighed her options – such as they were – Elinor wandered the garden paths, losing track of time. Eventually her agitation gave way to inertia, and then to lassitude, and she sank onto a stone bench at the furthest end of the garden. She was helpless, caught in a web. Why even attempt to escape? She would only break herself if she tried. Even the possibility of being a mistress was closed to her, now that Uncle Reginald was back in the picture.

Why hadn't she accepted Gus's offer when he'd made it? Now it was too late; no matter how many plots she tried to form, she could no longer escape her guardian. It seemed she was doomed to be the wife of a wine merchant...

Abruptly, she realized her breathing had quickened, her nape itched, and her body had tightened as if readying herself to run. She was being watched.

She turned slowly, expecting Uncle Reginald – though why he would approach her slowly and cautiously, she had no idea.

Gus stood only a few feet away. He was alone.

Elinor sank back onto the cold stone bench and

noticed for the first time that her seat offered a sweeping vista down the central aisle of the garden to the back facade of the house and on to the valley beyond. He must have spotted her the instant he'd left the house, but she'd been too lost in her thoughts to notice his approach.

"If you've come to collect me, Gus, I must tell you I have decided to become a garden statue. Just leave me here to freeze. I'll do my part by trying to maintain an attractive pose – and then Lord and Lady Burnside can have my corpse cast in bronze."

"Not a bad idea. Being immortalized in bronze, I mean. The other part sounds uncomfortable." He paused in front of her. "May I join you?"

Since Elinor was in a mood to seize any excuse for delay, she nodded. Even if it meant listening to his explanation of why she really must give up her odd notions and do as Uncle Reginald wanted, at least she could put the actual moment of surrender off for a little longer.

As Gus sat down beside her, he carefully hitched his buckskins so they didn't pull at the knee. He didn't look at her; he seemed to be trying to find words.

Elinor looked past him, across the garden and past the end of the house to the road beyond. A dusty cloud rolled across a field, thrown up by a fast-moving chaise. She wished she was riding in that carriage, going somewhere. *Anywhere.*

No, she didn't. How odd it all seemed! Only an hour ago, after their picnic had come to such an abrupt and unpleasant end, she had wanted nothing more than to get away from Gus. And yet here she sat – wishing, despite the chilly stone of the bench seeping into her bones and despite the awkwardness of their non-existent conversation, that she could stay beside him forever.

Forever.

She stifled a little gasp. She wanted forever – with him.

Under ordinary circumstances, she could have known Gus for months but not learned as much about him as she had in the short time since she had first laid eyes on him at Vauxhall Gardens. At a London ball, a girl might spend just a few minutes in any given evening waltzing with a particular gentleman. At that rate it would take years to accumulate the sort of intense time she had had with Gus – the hours they had spent talking and teasing and playing and flirting and sharing ... and loving.

I've fallen in love with him.

How foolish she had been, to let his charm overwhelm her defenses. But even as she accused herself, Elinor knew it was more than charm that had drawn her in. Izzy was the one who was star-struck by Lord Rake – by his mystique, his aura, his reputation. Elinor had grown to love Gus – the real man behind the mystique and the aura and the reputation.

She wondered if anyone in the world actually knew him as well as she did. Had he let the other women in his life spend as much time in his company? He might have taken those women to his bed, but had he allowed them to get as close to him as Elinor had? Had the other women shared the same sort of comfortable ease she had found with him?

Gus cleared his throat. "Aren't you going to ask why I came out here?"

She shrugged, trying to drag herself back to the moment. She would have plenty of time – the rest of her life, in fact – to think about how foolish it was to tumble into loving him. "Better you than Uncle Reginald. Did he send you? Or did you volunteer to come and fetch me?"

"Uncle Reginald is gone."

The words seemed to drop like a stone into a

fountain. Elinor couldn't get her breath – and even when the anchor in her chest finally started to melt away, she couldn't make herself believe she had heard correctly. "But he was so determined, so insistent. Why did he chase me all this way only to change his mind and give up?" Or maybe he hadn't given up, after all... Suspicion chewed at her. "What did you do, Gus?"

"I applied a little persuasion. He'll leave you alone now."

"But ..." she said uncertainly. "You told me you didn't pack your dueling pistols."

"I didn't need them. It seems Reginald wasn't quite as certain of the outcome as he implied. Despite what he told you, he harbors doubts whether your beloved–"

"*Don't* call him that."

"–Whether Mr. Dorrance would keep his bargain after all."

"I told you so!"

"In fact, he offered to sell you to me for the same sum Mr. Dorrance promised him in the marriage contracts."

Sell.

Elinor's mind was such an emotional stew that she could only begin to sort out what she was feeling. Revulsion at Uncle Reginald, of course – how dare he bargain for her as though she were a horse? Triumph, to know her instincts and her nagging suspicion of skullduggery had been correct after all. Gratitude at what seemed the narrowest possible escape from a future as an unwilling wife. Relief, of course, and buried down deep was even a strange glimmer of happiness.

So Uncle Reginald was truly gone. There was no need for the charade anymore, no need to stay longer at the hunting box. She was free to go on to Chichester and Miss Bradshaw's school – if it hadn't been for the inconvenient realization that her scandal-ridden presence there would not be welcome.

Except... Wariness tugged at her. "How did you answer him, Gus?"

"I accepted his bargain and sent him off to the village on one of Gerald's mounts."

He said it as easily as if the two actions were equivalent in his mind.

Maybe they're exactly the same. Buy a woman, loan a horse...

She couldn't bear to think about the first half of that statement – not just yet. So she focused on the other part. "Lord Burnside won't be pleased. You must not have seen the condition of the animal Uncle Reginald rode in on, if you let him take another."

"I doubt he'll be in such a hurry on the rest of his travels, so the horse will have an easier time of it. But I sent a groom along to make certain the animal is treated well and promptly returned. Uncle Reginald can rent a hack at the inn to get him back to London. Elinor—"

She still had a bit of pride – too much to allow her to be coerced. If the bargain had to be made, it was better that she be the one who offered it, rather than simply listening to his terms. "Then all we have left to discuss is the debt I owe you for rescuing me. I suppose it is foolish of me, but I wish I had accepted your offer before."

He frowned. "My offer?"

"To make me your mistress. I have only one way to pay what I owe, you see, but I wish it did not feel like we are making a business transaction of it."

Gus sucked in a deep breath. His face was grim.

Doubts tugged at her. "Or was that not what you were suggesting earlier, on our ride? Was it only other gentlemen you hoped might be interested in me?"

"Elinor, for god's sake, stop!" He leaped to his feet.

"I've thought it over, you see, while I've been sitting here." She must have done so, at any rate, for it was all perfectly clear to her now. "You are quite right. As a mistress, I can have a home of my own, with my... With my lover visiting only at my convenience – and his, of course. A wife has no choice – she must live with the same man until death parts them, even if they loathe each other. But if my lover displeases me, I can find another." She swallowed hard. "You were right about that as well, Gus. In the marriage market, I'm severely lacking."

"There is nothing wrong with you."

"But at least *some* gentlemen must prefer to take a mistress who knows how society works and how ladies behave. Tavern girls or actresses don't understand those things. They don't know how to run a house that a gentleman can be truly comfortable in, or how to put his friends at ease when they visit. I do." She laid her hand on his arm. His muscles were tense under her fingertips as she went on softly, "You're one of those gentlemen, aren't you, Gus? You could have any number of opera dancers or lightskirts. All you'd have to do is snap your fingers. But you wanted Delia. You wanted a lady."

She stood up, her breasts almost brushing his coat. Her knees were shaking, but she told herself that soon the most difficult part would be over. "I know I can't be Delia, but—"

She couldn't bring herself to say the words, so she stood on her toes and kissed him. Willing him to understand that she was offering everything she was and everything she had to give, she pressed herself against him, her arms around his neck, the tip of her tongue tracing his lips, trying her best to be seductive, asking him to kiss her in return.

But he stood like a rock. She might as well be embracing a block of granite.

Elinor kissed him a second time, slowly – for it was the only goodbye she would allow herself – and let her arms drop. "I see I was wrong again. I do beg your pardon."

On unsteady feet, she fled toward the house without looking back. She heard him call out, but her ears were pounding with exertion and embarrassment, and she refused to pause.

The nearest entrance was through one of the long windows standing ajar between the terrace and the drawing room. At least if she went in that way she would not immediately face servants coming and going; she could take a moment to gather herself.

Hampered by the long skirt of the riding habit, she was breathless by the time she reached the top of the terrace stairs. As she tugged at the window, Gus caught up with her, his longer stride eating up the distance.

Elinor refused to look at him as she pulled the window open. "If you're worried about what I'll do now, Gus, you needn't concern yourself. I ask only for transportation to the village, where I will seek work as a chambermaid at the inn. Surely sooner or later a gentleman staying there will find me appealing enough to offer me his protection – and eventually I will be able to pay my debt." She stepped into the drawing room.

"Damn it, Elinor!" Gus was half a step behind her, and when Elinor paused to let her eyes adjust to the more muted light inside the drawing room, he seized her arm and swung her around to face him. But instead of speaking, he groaned, pulled her tightly against him, and kissed her – a long, deep, demanding and utterly terrifying kiss. A kiss that said he had lost all control and had no intention of even attempting to regain it.

Elinor would have sworn the floor swayed under her feet, but perhaps that was just the effect of her knees turning to jelly. She was clinging to him for support – certainly not because she wanted to encourage him. What was wrong with the man, anyway? If he was going to kiss her at all, why hadn't he responded when she kissed him in the garden?

Don't lie to yourself. You don't care why. The important thing was that he was kissing her now, as though he intended to consume her – and with her last coherent thought, Elinor swore to do her best to make sure he never stopped.

A small, polite cough interrupted, and a gravelly voice said, "You see, Delia? I did tell you Rake had gotten himself into deep water. I believe I have won our bet."

Even through the haze surrounding Elinor, the voice was unmistakable. She had last heard it in Grosvenor Square, right after Gus had first kissed her. But what was Lady Stone doing here? And had she said *Delia*?

Elinor was afraid to turn her head to look. If the very woman whom Gus really wanted was standing only a few feet away...

He's mine, she wanted to shout – as though saying it aloud would make it true.

Another familiar, more feminine voice answered. "I'm not convinced of anything yet, ma'am. As for you, Gus... You actually brought your *chere amie* to my own house?"

Her own house? But if that was the case, then Delia was also Lady Burnside. Had Gus been planning to run away to the continent with the wife of his closest friend? – the same woman who had installed Mrs. Pollack at the hunting box to restore order and morals to a house it seemed had had neither?

Elinor's head was spinning. The situation defied logic in so many ways she couldn't even begin to add them up.

"Elinor is not my *chere amie*." Gus's voice was rough, and Elinor's last hope – a hope so feeble she hadn't even recognized she was holding onto it – died.

Delia laughed. "If you're going to try to convince me I imagined that kiss... Is she wearing my riding habit?"

Elinor managed to look past Gus's shoulder long enough to confirm that the dark-haired woman standing in the middle of the room was indeed the beauty who had been in the Vauxhall Gardens folly with him.

She pushed herself away from Gus and turned to face the beauty. "Lord Rackham is telling the truth. I'm not his – well, his *anything*, really. My apologies, Lady Burnside, for–" She swallowed, but her throat was so dry it hurt. *For trying to steal the man who loves you.* "For everything. I needed shelter, you see, and Gus... Lord Rackham, I mean... I had no idea it was your..."

Delia was studying her with lips pursed and forehead furrowed.

Since she seemed only to be making things worse, Elinor stopped trying and turned to the older woman with a small curtsy. "Lady Stone, if I might beg a word with you in private?"

The old woman's beady eyes shone brighter. "Of course, my dear. Let's sit down for a good gossip – I'd love to have you fill me in."

"Oh, no," Gus said, and reached for Elinor's arm. "You are not to cozen her into telling you anything, ma'am."

"My dear Rake," Lady Stone said cheerfully, "keeping a lady next to you by force is hardly a romantic gesture. Do take Delia for a walk in the garden and mend your fences. You seem to have a lot to explain."

Gus looked as though he intended to argue. Elinor dodged his hand and darted toward Lady Stone. "We could go to another room, my lady."

"No, for the butler will be bringing me a glass of port any moment now – to cut the dust of travel, you know. We had only just arrived when you burst in."

Then the two ladies must have been in the carriage Elinor had spotted from the garden. It didn't really matter, she supposed.

Lady Stone settled into the corner of a settee and patted the seat beside her. "Come and sit, child. Oh, Rake?" she called after Gus. "You might do me a favor and convince Delia she really must not renege on a wager." She smiled at Elinor. "I do hope she has sufficient funds on hand. It was rather a sizable bet."

Elinor was longing to know how much Delia Burnside had wagered – and on precisely what. But asking would be only a feeble attempt to distract herself from the important and difficult conversation she had requested. Now that the moment had arrived, however, she had trouble finding words. Was it foolish of her even to imagine Lady Stone could – or would – help her?

"I know I am being very forward," she said finally. "And I realize, after what you saw in Grosvenor Square, my name may already be so blackened that nothing can repair the damage."

"Blackened? Surely you are not implying I have deliberately ruined a young lady with gossip?" Lady Stone sounded almost haughty.

But there was the hint of a twinkle in those beady black eyes, giving Elinor hope. "I am certain Gus is correct when he says you have the power to do so."

"Indeed I do. But go ahead and ask, child. What is it you want?"

Elinor's voice cracked. "Is it possible you might help me find some honorable employment?"

Lady Stone's eyebrows jerked upward. "I believe your last career plan was to be a chambermaid with a hope of advancing to mistress."

"You must know I said that only because I was angry at Gus."

"So much, my dear, was apparent. The reason for your fury, however, is less clear. Has he behaved himself badly? Threatened you?" Her voice dropped. "Forced you?"

"Oh, no! No, Gus wouldn't do that."

"Well, I didn't think it likely, or he wouldn't have let me discover where he'd taken you."

Elinor had opened her mouth to return to her question, but the announcement made her jaw drop. "I wondered how you found us, but – *Gus told you?*"

"Not quite. His groom brought a message for me back to town along with the bays Rake was driving when you left Grosvenor Square. It was easy enough to persuade the groom to tell me where you'd gone. Of course then I had to rush right out to see what was afoot – and Delia insisted on coming as soon as she heard he was retreating to her house."

No wonder Lady Burnside was feeling out of sorts. And no wonder Gus had sounded as though someone had clubbed him. He must have contacted Lady Stone to find out what Delia's reaction had been to the news. But he couldn't have anticipated she would come racing across country to see for herself... or that she would rip into him, rather than shedding heartbroken tears, when she arrived.

Biggs tapped on the door and came in with a decanter. "Your port, my lady. Shall I bring you something, miss?"

Elinor shook her head. Lady Stone filled the second glass on the tray and handed it to her. "Drink," she ordered. "It's good for you when you've had a shock. I'll give your question some consideration. I do occasionally hear of a lady who needs a companion."

"I don't suppose *you*..." Elinor's voice trailed off.

"You think I might wish to hire someone to follow me around? It's an interesting idea, to be sure, but I doubt it would work out."

Elinor knew it had been a feeble hope – but she'd had to try. At least Lady Stone knew the worst and wouldn't hold it against her.

"In any case, here comes Delia through the garden, and since I am certain you would rather not be in the same room with her just now, perhaps you should run along, my dear."

"What? Oh – certainly." Elinor set her half-filled glass back on the tray and slipped out into the entry hall. She'd go up to her room, she decided. No one except Betsy would bother her there, and a good cry certainly couldn't hurt.

As she passed the study on her way to the stairway, the door swung wide. Gus's hands closed on her arms, pulling her into the room. He nudged the door closed with his hip and stood looking down at her.

"I don't..." Elinor's voice was breathy and far higher than usual. "How did you get here? You were in the garden with Lady Burnside."

"Our conversation didn't take long."

"That doesn't sound promising – even though all you had to do was explain to her that I mean nothing to you." She tipped her head to one side and regarded him. "But you didn't tell her, did you? Honestly, Gus, if you expect *me* to convince her..."

"You've done enough damage already." He sounded grim.

"Now that is simply unfair! To blame me for how it's all turned out is – well, it's outrageous. You're the one who kissed *me*, so it's no wonder if Delia isn't inclined to accept your excuses. It was just your good luck Cousin Reginald didn't see anything of the sort, or he'd have pushed for you to marry me."

Gus said softly, "Indeed it was my good luck."

Elinor's eyes filled with tears, and she turned away

so he wouldn't see them.

"Because if he had tried to force the issue, you would never believe I do this of my own free will." He captured her hands and dropped to one knee before her. "Elinor, will you marry me?"

She thought for a moment that her heart had actually stopped, she was so stunned. "What is wrong with you, Gus?"

"Not exactly the response a man hopes for when he finally decides to ask that question."

"Well, if you're raising the stakes so Delia will take you seriously, I'd advise you to be more cautious. I might actually accept, and then where would you be? Oh, do get up off the floor – what if someone came in and saw you kneeling there?"

"Not until I have an answer."

"Then *no* – just as I told you earlier. By the way, it's hardly flattering to ask a woman for her hand when she's already assured you she would refuse." But her insides were fluttering madly. *Convince me, Gus. Please – convince me.*

Gus rose, dusting off the knee of his buckskins. "That's why I didn't ask a few minutes ago in the garden, when I came out to find you after Uncle Reginald left. I intended to, but—"

"Then he did pressure you? Made you feel you must offer for me?"

"No. He told me he expected I would never think of marrying you. He insulted you – and made me realize I've been thinking of marrying you almost from the moment we met. I just wasn't wise enough to see what was happening. You've ruined me, Elinor."

"A scandal like this one will only burnish your reputation, Lord Rake."

"That's not what I mean. Every minute I have spent with you has made me more reluctant to go back to my old life. You are unique, and you are vastly entertaining. You are kind and talented and witty and loveable and sensual. I wanted to seduce you, to make you mine for a while. But that's not enough. I want everything – and I cannot settle for less."

"What about Delia?" Her voice was little more than a breath. "Are you her lover?"

"She is so madly in love with her husband that she'd laugh at the very idea. Gerald was busy with his negotiations on a bill in the House of Lords that night, so he stuck me with escort duty because Delia wanted to go to Vauxhall."

Elinor frowned. "Then you didn't mean for her to run away with you?"

"People in the *ton* flirt, my dear. It was a game, that's all."

She thought back to the conversation in the folly – the lazy tone of Delia's voice, the way she had playfully smacked Gus's hand with her fan, the fact she hadn't taken offense at the things he'd said about her husband – and a little knot in the center of Elinor's chest eased.

"And that's what I expected when I agreed to help you, too," Gus went on. "A game. A way to pass the time. An amusing few hours."

"But then Uncle Reginald came along and you couldn't get rid of me."

"By then I didn't want to see the last of you – but I soon realized I was holding a double-edged sword. You put your faith in me to protect you, but the more you trusted me, the more I wanted to make love to you. To make you want me as much as I wanted you."

She started to speak, but he laid a gentle finger across her lips.

"I know it's not very flattering that it took me so long to recognize what was really happening," he said softly, "and it was only Uncle Reginald's stupid assumption that woke me up. But with every smile and every artless confidence and every word you spoke to me, I fell a little more in love with you. So I ask you again, Elinor – will you be my wife?"

She hoped he couldn't hear the tremor in her voice. "If you actually married me, the talk would go on forever about how foolish you were to fall into a trap set by a conniving, managing female."

"No one will know. It seems I was mistaken about Lady Stone – she treasures her reputation as a gossip more than she enjoys actually spreading tittle-tattle. She didn't even tell Delia about the kiss."

Elinor shook her head. "But you didn't know when you sent her a message that she would be discreet."

"No, I didn't. But you should have been safely in Chichester long before the gossip could spread so far. When the situation changed, I convinced myself it worth the risk to ask Lady Stone to keep what she had seen to herself."

"And if she hadn't?"

"It would have been my fault, if you were ruined. I think, when I sent the message, part of me already knew I wanted to keep you forever – no matter what it took. If she had told the world, then you would have to stay with me."

"But since she didn't – Gus, this means I can go to Miss Bradshaw's school after all." Had everything he said been mere pretty words? Despite it all, would he seize the opportunity to escape?

"You could, except – have you forgotten? – I own you now. Just ask your Uncle Reginald. And therefore you must do as I say." He kissed her fingertips and reminded, "You did tell me once that when persuasion doesn't work, I should escalate to threats."

"And you told me you'd never be caught in parson's mousetrap."

"Walking in, fully aware of what I want, is a very different thing than being caught." He cupped her face in his hands. "I'm certain about this, Elinor. I want to marry you. But if you are not convinced, then I'll court you – even if it means setting myself up next door to your school until you're persuaded."

She looked into his eyes. There was no humor there, not even a hint of the teasing gleam she had grown so used to. She missed that outrageous sparkle – and yet, the intense seriousness in his expression was the only thing that could have satisfied her. "Well, when you put it like that..." she said slowly.

The rest of her answer was lost against his mouth as he swept her close, and the fluttery feeling in Elinor's stomach spread through every inch of her body as he kissed her. Finally, breathlessly, she managed to say, "Don't you want to know what changed my mind?"

"You'll be a countess." Gus turned his attention to the hollow at the base of her throat.

"Oh – that's true, isn't it? I hadn't stopped to think."

"It's not the title? Then it's because I'm rich."

"How can you think that of me, Gus?"

"Perhaps you want to sail off on my yacht?"

"I'd forgotten the yacht. Can we really go to Italy and Greece and—"

He stopped kissing her. "It's because you take such delight in upsetting my plans and my life, isn't it?"

"Not at all. It's because of the book you loaned me." She wriggled happily and tipped her head back. "It felt really nice when you kissed my throat, Gus."

He didn't take the hint. "The book?"

"It's a three-volume novel, but you only let me take me the first one. The others must still be on the shelf in your library. So if I'm ever to finish reading the story–"

"Minx." He picked her up and spun her around

until her head was muzzy and she was breathless with laughter.

"Do you still care about the story?" he demanded.

"Well – not very much." She flung her arms around his neck and kissed him soundly. "Oh, Gus –I do love you. And of course I'll marry you." The words – words she had thought she'd never say – tickled her tongue with happiness.

Gus smiled. "Before or after I seduce you?" Rather than waiting for an answer, he carried her over to the wing-backed chair by the fire, settled her on his lap, and set about doing exactly that.

About the Author

Leigh Michaels (leighmichaels.com) is the award-winning author of more than 100 books, including Regency romances, contemporary romances, and non-fiction. Six of her books have been finalists in the Romance Writers of America RITA contest, and more than 35 million copies of her books are in print in 25 languages and 120 countries.

She is also the author of *On Writing Romance* and teaches romance writing online at Gotham Writers' Workshop.

Her Regency romances include:

The Birthday Scandal
An Affair for the Season
The Wedding Affair
Just One Season in London
The Mistress' House
Wedding Daze

Made in the USA
Monee, IL
05 January 2022

86986263R00080